SENSUAL GAMES

ELITE HEIRS OF MANHATTAN BOOK 5

MISSY WALKER

Copyright © 2024 by Missy Walker

All rights reserved.

No part of this publication may be reproduced, distributed or transmitted in any form or by any means, including by any electronic or mechanical means, including photocopying, recording or information storage and retrieval systems, without prior written consent from the author, except for the use of brief quotations in a book review.

Cover Design: Missy Walker

Editor: Swish Design & Editing

Who runs the world?
Girls.

Elite *Men* Of Manhattan and
Elite *Heirs* of Manhattan Family Tree

BARRETT BLACK LOURDE DIAMOND	CONNOR DIAMOND PEPPER LITTLE	ARI GOLDSMITH OLIVIA WILLOWS	MAGNUS MILLER EVELYN BLACK
FORBIDDEN LUST #1 **FORBIDDEN LOVE #2**	**LOST LOVE #3**	**MISSING LOVE #4**	**GUARDED LOVE #5**

| COLTON BLACK | LUCIAN DIAMOND | ROSE GOLDSMITH | NOAH GOLDSMITH | ARIA MILLER | VALENTINA MILLER | MILES YOUNG |

| SIENNA BLACK |

SEDUCTIVE HEARTS #1
COLTON AND ROSE

SWEET SURRENDER #2
NOAH AND SIENNA

SINFUL DESIRES #3
ARIA AND MILES

SILENT CRAVINGS #4
VALENTINA AND EVAN

SENSUAL GAMES #5
IVY & LUCIAN

1

LUCIAN

A one-night stand had come back to haunt me.

Of all days.

Here I was, on the verge of taking my so-called rightful position in my family's media empire, and a woman, who I would've been glad to see again under other circumstances, happened to be someone with her sights on my job.

While I wasn't exactly thrilled over the idea of taking a leadership position in the family company, I didn't want to fuck things up on the first day my entire team assembled, either. It was bad enough I had to deal with being my father's only child. *"The Diamond name is a legacy. It is your responsibility to carry the family name."*

Lucky me.

Granted, it was a good name, a respected one. I could've done a lot worse.

Today was supposed to be the first step in proving to the great Connor Diamond I had what it took to carry on in his footsteps one day. Most men his age would have been interested in retiring, at least partly, but he was as hands-on as ever and had led the way during the acquisition of a failing media company. One of those old, barely limping behemoths left behind in the wake of social media, digital imprints, and lessening subscriptions as more and more information became easily accessible online. They weren't willing to pivot or weren't able to. Either way, the result was the same, leading us to this moment. It was hardly the first time Dad had absorbed another company into ours, extending its reach, extending his influence and power.

But it was the first time I played a part, so naturally, a one-night stand had to show herself at this pivotal moment in my so-called career.

Not only a one-night stand. That alone, I could have handled. It was the fact we'd be working together. That was Dad's code for *I don't want you fucking things up on your own*. For twenty-five years, he had looked over my shoulder, always waiting for me to make a wrong move and tarnish his precious reputation. The stakes were higher now, with me sitting at the helm of the company's digital division. Not that I had the first clue what it meant to run a division or be the vice president of anything, which he knew damn well. I still couldn't understand why he had named me for the position with no experience to my name beyond a few summers interning with the company and nothing much else in between.

As far as he was concerned, all I needed was somebody to watch over me and make sure I didn't blow up anything. No one had to say it out loud. I knew the way the man's mind worked.

I should have known this was all too good to be true. I hadn't asked for the job, and I didn't want it. That didn't mean my pride could handle a babysitter.

Especially not a babysitter I had fucked for hours until

Sensual Games 3

we were both drenched in sweat and exhausted to the point of passing out in a tangle of arms and legs on a half-striped bed. We hadn't exactly been careful to keep the room in one piece. It was the kind of night I wouldn't forget anytime soon.

Did that mean I had to remember every damn time I came to work? Talk about a productivity killer. At the moment, she was looking at me from the corner of her eye, seated at the end of the first row of chairs assembled in our conference room for this welcome meeting. Dad sat to my left, and somehow, he managed to make it look like he was paying attention to the orientation video playing on the screen in front of us. I had watched it a few times during its development and knew we were coming to the end, meaning it would soon be time for me to deliver my prepared address.

My attention shifted to my right, and her head snapped around until she was facing forward. Good thing she chose this profession instead of acting, considering she was shit at acting like my gaze didn't shake her up. She had recognized me right away, though who could blame her after I'd given her an unforgettable night?

"Right here." I swept the dresser free of cologne and the other toiletries I'd left out while getting ready for the wedding. Bottles and tubes hit the floor while I lifted her and placed her on the surface, tearing off my tie and jacket as she worked my shirt buttons. She looked up at me, and the animal hunger blazing behind her gray eyes left me claiming her mouth, thrusting my tongue inside while I stripped off everything to feel more of her touch.

I was no stranger to getting caught up in lust after finding somebody I clicked with, but this? This was downright baffling. Not that I wanted to think about it at the moment, especially with most of the blood in my brain having traveled south to harden my cock.

She leaned against me while opening my shirt, her mouth trailing across my chest and turning my blood to fire. I reached behind her to slide the zipper of her dress down to her waist. The creamy tits I'd admired for hours while we flirted during the reception were barely encased in lace, the material soft under my palms when I fondled her, burying my face between them, growling as I tasted and plundered.

"Oh, yes, please..." Her sweet, helpless whimpers were music to my ears— what man alive didn't want to hear a woman like her falling apart because of them? Satisfaction swelled in me, demanded more. More touch, more taste, more everything.

Dad's elbow to my side startled me out of my memory. The presentation was over, and somebody had flipped on the lights. It was my turn to get up and do a little dance for my father's approval.

Thankfully, there was a podium to stand behind and a folder full of notes I could hold in front of me to hide the semi that started to grow, thanks to poor timing. What was I supposed to do? I'd been completely blindsided by the memories.

I wasn't asking for this. I didn't want her here, now.

The entire point of a one-night stand was for it to last *one* night.

"Good morning." I offered a brief smile I hoped would cover up any awkwardness I was fighting to contain. Was it enough? My father peered up at me, wearing the sort of expression he saved for private, one-on-one moments. *Do not fuck this up. Do not make me regret giving you this chance.* He may as well have been holding up a sign with those words printed across the front, along with a few other unflattering additions. Yet, to an outsider, he was a respected businessman and philanthropist who had done a lot of good with his power and influence.

Determination injected energy into my voice. "As you heard in the presentation, which just wrapped up, we do take the concept of family seriously here." Pitiful, corporate bullshit. *Family.* No matter how many times I told Dad to stop harping on the concept, trying to help him understand people didn't buy that pandering bullshit anymore, he refused to listen. It was one of the only areas where he had insisted on getting his way during my speech.

"We understand there might be growing pains. We are here for you, day or night, and hope you will feel comfortable sharing any concerns with us. We respect the corporate culture you left and don't expect a simple, overnight transition. These things take time, and I know you'll find everyone here is reasonable, understanding, and more than willing to work together for the greater good. The way any family does."

God, I wanted to gag. Why not have me up here in a pair of tap shoes while we were at it so I could add a little entertainment? I caught more than a few people rolling their eyes as I droned on, and I couldn't blame them. It wasn't their fault they were able to see through this ridiculous farce.

That almost platinum hair kept catching the light overhead, drawing my attention time and again. She sat upright, hands folded in her lap, her eyes trained squarely on me. *"So big... so good..."* I ground my molars, tearing my gaze from her when Dad softly cleared his throat. Whether he did it because he noticed me losing track of my thoughts or not, I had no idea.

"After final remarks offered by our CEO, you will be directed to your new workstations throughout the building, on your division's respective floors," I continued, deliberately looking anywhere but at her. Did she know who I was at the wedding? Was she on to me all the time? Was our night together her way of scoring points? Fucking me in hopes of getting a head start on the new job?

A sour taste filled my mouth and left me reaching for the bottle of water on the podium, taking a sip in hopes of washing the bitterness away.

"And please remember," I concluded, practically racing for the finish line in hopes of putting an end to all of this. "My door is always open. I look forward to my first meeting with the new digital team early next week. For now, get your feet wet, orient yourselves, and don't forget to ask questions whenever they come up. We are here to help you make this transition as smooth and painless as possible. Thank you all very much for being here with us, and I look forward to working with all of you."

They were smart enough to offer polite applause before I nodded to Dad. "Now, a few words from our CEO. Be careful," I warned, dropping my voice to something barely above a whisper. "You better sit up straight and be on your best behavior, but then that's probably the command only reserved for me when I was getting yelled at back in the day." Laughter filled the room while Dad shook his head and wagged a finger at me. "If I were you, I would be on the safe side," I finished, and a fresh wave of laughter resulted when I stepped aside to let Dad take my place.

We exchanged a glance, and then I returned to my seat. *I set it up. All you have to do is bring it home.*

Now that the part I had dreaded most was over—my first time being paraded around like this, forced to play happy boss in front of a bunch of strangers—I could sit back in my chair and, once again, go over the situation I had found myself in.

But instead of thinking about what Ivy's presence meant for my job security, where did my mind go? Right back to my hotel room, around the time I pulled her off the dresser and fell onto the bed with her underneath me.

I couldn't keep my hands off her, touching everything I could reach while tasting every inch of her skin. There was something wild, almost unhinged, about it, a sense of complete abandon. Everybody knew women tended to get horny as hell at weddings —at least, that was the way I'd always found it. This was on another level. Every touch, every high-pitched whimper and deep, throaty moan was a challenge. Could I make her do it again? And would she do it louder this time?

"As my son told you," Dad offered, nodding toward me. "Family is something we focus on here. And please, don't get me wrong," he continued with a soft chuckle. "I'm not trying to blow smoke up anyone's rear. There's no such thing as a complete work-life balance. I know that too well, myself. Sometimes, life takes precedence, while other times, we make sacrifices to advance ourselves professionally. I don't expect anyone to walk in here every day and be able to completely disconnect from the life they left outside these doors. It's impossible. And it's unfair to demand that. But don't get me wrong. We do work hard…"

This would be challenging enough to pay attention to if I wasn't out of my mind trying to focus on anything but this insane twist of fate, if it was indeed a twist and not something Ivy had orchestrated. I knew I had to be stronger than this, but nothing could stop me from sliding a glance her way, gauging her reaction. She may as well have been some lovesick kid, hanging onto Dad's every word as she gazed up at him.

Damn, she was gorgeous. Not that I could forget, but remembering something and seeing it in front of me were two different things. Her delicate features were perfectly balanced, but it was the eyes that drew me in. They had from the first second I had spotted her sitting at the bar in the clubhouse dining room, where some of the guests had spilled over to take a break from the music and dancing. The second those orbs had landed on me, shining and sharp, I was a fish on a hook. All she had to do was reel me in, and an inviting smile had done that.

Looking back, I cringed at myself. Had I really made it that easy for her? How was I supposed to know we would meet again and under these circumstances?

But she had to know. The takeover hadn't exactly happened overnight. There had already been rumblings in the air. I was one of the groomsmen, for fuck's sake. My name was in the program everybody received before the wedding. She had to know who I was by the time I'd introduced myself.

I thought I had picked her up and seduced her, but now I was seeing everything clearly. It had been the other way around. She had used me. She thought she could take my job. A job I hadn't wanted when I woke up that morning but was now the most important thing in my world.

She wanted to play games? That was fine with me. Nobody tried to take what was mine and got away with it. And she was about to find that out.

Dad clapped his hands together briskly, snapping me to attention. "Now, as Lucian explained, you'll all be gathered together and taken to your new workstations. When you reach them, you'll find copies of the employee handbook, along with welcome packages we assembled for each of you. Again, I look forward to working with you, and we hope you can be as happy and as fulfilled here as you were before

Diamond Media and Jones Media joined forces. Thank you all very much."

He headed straight for me, and I stood, aware of the icy blonde watching us. "Well, this is it," Dad murmured. "Tomorrow, you'll be working one-on-one with Ivy, showing her the ropes. She'll take on a managerial role, a step down from her prior title but with better compensation."

"What a shame I had no idea I had to do any of that," I muttered, offering a tight smile to some rando who caught my eye as he walked past. Somebody sucking up, trying to get me to remember their face. Like that would help them if they couldn't hack moving up to the big leagues.

"If that was an oversight, it was on your part." Dad's narrowed eyes found me and locked on. All I could do was withstand the weight of his disappointment. "I sent you the list of new employees and their past positions. Since when can you not add two and two together?"

This motherfucker. My blood was boiling, and I wanted nothing more than to throw his bullshit job in his face, along with the thinly veiled contempt he'd always held for me. It was a shame he had only been granted one child, and that child happened to be me. Someone he couldn't trust to work on their own. Somebody he had to assign a handler to.

"It's fine," I assured him, fighting to maintain composure if only to defy his expectations. "We can talk about the strategy I've come up with during our breakfast meeting on Wednesday." Two days from now, I would more than likely have a better idea of what I was dealing with when it came to her.

"Fair enough." He turned away, all smiles for a pair of older women who obviously couldn't resist his charm. Women never could, especially the ones closer to his age.

I was not in the mood to charm anyone, especially not

when I found Ivy lingering in the doorway, staring my way, one eyebrow arched. *More like Poison Ivy. Nice to look at, dangerous as all fuck to touch.*

She was not going to take this from me. I would see to it she regretted ever thinking she could. I might have let my dick do the thinking for me once, but I wouldn't make that mistake again.

2

IVY

"I brought these because I know they're your favorite." I buried my nose deep in the fragrant blooms I'd finished arranging on Mom's windowsill. They were gorgeous and had cost more than I wanted to think about, but she needed a little cheer in this bleak, dingy room.

I turned away from the vase of roses, my gaze landing on what looked suspiciously like mouse droppings in the corner. Over the months, I'd seen more than a few mouse traps here in the only nursing facility I could afford, and while my stomach soured, I had no choice but to turn a blind eye. Aside from lodging complaints with the state advocate, there was nothing else I could do to try to improve Mom's situation. I needed her taken care of so I could go out and work. But it was a vicious cycle. I worked so I could keep her here.

Taking a seat at her bedside, I pulled her hairbrush from the drawer in the nightstand. Her energy was low today. Normally, she at least tried to be awake when I came to visit, but she didn't have it in her tonight.

Instead of trying to wake her up, I leaned in and

unwound the long, silver braid hanging over one shoulder. Bits of food were stuck in her hair, which nobody had bothered to clean out after she'd eaten. Another thing I had to overlook. My soul was weary as I began brushing her soft locks.

"I'll be making more here than I ever did at Jones Media," I told her, and for once, I could let a little excitement leak into my voice. Not only would I be making more, but I would be making enough to afford an actual, decent facility in Hoboken. It wouldn't be the Ritz, but it was clean, and the staff seemed kind and on top of things. She wouldn't have to feel like she was simply waiting to die after her stroke.

I brushed slowly, remembering how soothing it always was when she used to do this for me when I was a little. Even when Dad walked out on us, and Mom struggled with bare cupboards and empty pockets, she still brushed my hair every night. "You should see the offices," I whispered as I worked. "I swear, it's like something you would see in a movie. Great big offices with all these windows so far above the city. They have an on-site masseuse, Mom. Can you believe it? I thought my eyes were going to fall out of my head when they showed us the gym and the sauna right there in the building for anybody to use. They have actual, professional cooks come in to prepare breakfast and lunch, so we don't even have to leave if we don't want to, but we can," I continued. "It's up to us. I know I sound easy to impress, but come on. It's like a whole different world than where I came from."

Something made me wrinkle my nose, though, and it wasn't the pervasive, underlying odor of urine that always filled the air. It was the memory of a certain pair of smoldering eyes, so dark they were almost black and so piercing they practically stared into my soul. Of all the people to show up in my life, it had to be *him.* Lucian Diamond. He, of the huge dick and magic tongue.

He remembered me as clearly as I remembered him. Though we hadn't exchanged more than a few words in front of his dad, I felt it as plain as anything. He knew who I was, knew why I was there, and for some reason, he seemed to resent me.

Not that it mattered. I was used to being resented by the men I had to work alongside, who thought the whole world should be handed to them just because they had a dick hanging between their legs. It's like that was some great accomplishment. Forget those of us who had to work twice as hard to get half as far as they did.

I caught myself grinding my teeth until my jaw ached, then forced myself to loosen up. "It looks like I'll be working with the boss's son," I told Mom, gazing at her beautiful, slightly unfamiliar face. The stroke had weakened her muscles, and there were times I was startled by how old and helpless she looked. I kept expecting to find my mom, the woman I'd always known—vibrant, bright, sharp as a tack.

A familiar stinging sensation started behind my eyes that left me blinking back hot, painful tears. One second, she was fine, and the next, I was scrambling around, trying to figure out what would happen next. How was I supposed to take care of her when I could barely afford to take care of myself?

"He's pretty cute," I told her, remembering all the talks we had at the kitchen table when I was a kid, crushing on one boy or another. The word didn't come close to touching the truth. "Okay, he's ridiculously handsome. I met him before. Isn't life weird? He was at Rose Goldsmith's wedding. Remember her? I did that piece about her a few years ago when she decided to quit modeling so she could work full-time in her family business. We really hit it off, and she's a great girl. Turns out, she knows this guy. Lucian Diamond."

And I slept with him.

I probably wouldn't have if I'd known we'd end up working together, but that was the way my life went. Like somebody up there got off on throwing curveballs and watching me scramble to hit them.

Even saying his name sent a ripple of pleasure down my spine. It had only been a handful of weeks since that early June wedding. Time couldn't make me forget how magical it was or how hot it was, and it was extremely hot. Even sitting here in a room that smelled of urine and mouse droppings, I somehow managed to get a little wet at the memory.

"So fucking tight." He closed his eyes, grunting like he was trying to hold on and was failing miserably. All because of me, because he liked the way it felt inside me. This absolute god, this gorgeous, charismatic man with a body most women would kill for the chance to touch, losing his grip on himself, all because of the grip I had on his dick.

A dick that felt like it was going to rip me in half, but I loved it. Fuck, I craved more. I may as well have never had sex before this. It felt that new. All I could do was hold on tight, gripping him with my legs around his hips while he took me hard, mercilessly, urged on by the helpless cries he tore out of me.

The memory of his deep, primal grunts had me tingling by the time I stood.

I pushed away the memory as I refilled the empty water cup before leaning over and whispering, " I'd better go." Pressing my lips to Mom's forehead, I arranged the blankets over her, making sure her phone and her remote control were nearby for when she woke up. "I love you. It won't be much longer until I can get you out of here, I promise."

I doubted she could hear me, but I believed there was still some part of her that could hear me in her dreams. That was all I had. Hope. And even that was starting to run a little thin.

It didn't matter. I wasn't going to sit around and wait to be rescued. This wasn't a fairy tale. I would have to rescue myself and my mother along with me. Nobody was going to stop me.

IT WAS NEVER EARLY ENOUGH to take the subway and have it be empty enough to get a little peace. People were everywhere, pushing me around on the platform, then elbowing me as I gripped a metal bar to keep my balance while we whizzed through dark tunnels. Not that I wasn't used to it. One of the rites of passage when it came to living in New York was learning to navigate the subway. Mom always used to tell me stories of how things were even worse when she was younger, which I'd found hard to believe until seeing pictures of the way things used to look when she was my age. The city was at least trying to make things nicer than they were back then.

Still, there was nothing like climbing out of the tunnel and breathing fresh air, at least as fresh as it could be in early July when it was already humid as hell and only seven in the morning.

The sight of my building up ahead and the promise of air conditioning carried me over the sidewalk in the worn-out flats I put on to get to and from work. A pair of carefully maintained pumps sat in my shoulder bag—I would leave them at my desk at the end of the day now that I had a desk to get settled in.

We weren't supposed to report for work until nine, but I believed in the old adage of the early bird getting the worm. If Lucian didn't like the idea of us working together for some personal reason, I had to do everything in my power to change his mind. I needed this too badly. It had to work out. Things were awkward enough without having to look over my shoulder and hope the owner's son wasn't somehow insulted by my existence.

Not that he struck me as being that childish when we met. Far from it. I wouldn't have slept with him if he came off as some spoiled little jerk. I had no desire to waste my time on somebody like that, even for one night.

Stepping out of the elevator, I wasn't surprised to find the floor mostly empty. Anticipation made the blood hum in my veins and left my skin tingling as I explored the large break room where a pair of cooks set up a hot breakfast buffet. There was also a refrigerator with a clear door that revealed cups of yogurt, smoothies, hard-boiled eggs, and fruit salad. I snagged a smoothie before continuing past clusters of cubicles where some of my old coworkers would sit now that we were expected to settle into our new positions.

I wouldn't be in a cubicle, and I didn't know how to feel about it. My desk sat outside the corner office of Lucian Diamond, the way so many assistants sat outside their boss's office. He wasn't my boss, was he? No. His dad, the man who signed my paycheck, wanted *me* to show his son the ropes.

His son, who now crossed his glass-walled office, was plainly visible as he took a seat at a sleek, black desk. A leather sofa sat at the far end of the room, opposite the desk, along with a pair of matching chairs and a long coffee table. Aside from a handful of plants like those found elsewhere on the floor, there were no personal touches. There hadn't been time to consider that yet, I realized. He was that green.

He liked to come in early. The man managed to surprise me. There I was, assuming he would roll in around ten, maybe eleven, being the boss's son.

I barely had time to process it when his obscene good looks erased everything else from my mind. It didn't help that I'd always had a thing for guys who looked like they had a chip on their shoulder, brooding and smoldering. The man smoldered, that was for sure. It was surprising my skin didn't blister in the heat.

When his attention landed on me, standing like an idiot next to my desk and gaping at him like every brain cell spontaneously died, the heat damn near singed my hair. Those eyes. They had the power to stop my heart.

And when they narrowed, they got my pulse racing in a dangerous way. There he was, resenting me. Why? What the hell had I done to deserve this attitude?

Do not let him ruin this.

Too many men had made me lose my cool in the past. Until now, I'd been lucky enough to keep my job in spite of my temper. There was a reason I made myself indispensable. Nobody wanted to fire the girl who always swooped in to save the day. So what if she had a sharp tongue and refused to suffer fools?

My shoulders rolled back, and my chin lifted. I left my bag on my currently empty desk and strode up to the door separating us. "Good morning," I offered with a smile. Was it obvious I couldn't help but hear his voice in my head? *"Do you like that? Does my cock make that tight pussy feel good?"*

Get it together. That was weeks ago.

This was now when we were both fully dressed and most definitely not in the throes of passion.

"Good morning." Ugh, why did his deep voice have to bring velvet to mind? Rich, warm, sexy as hell. "You're here early. Any special reason?"

I could've done without the heavy dose of suspicion in his voice. "Is it a crime to come in early on my first full day on the job?" I asked.

"Aren't you a hard worker?" He folded his hands on top of his desk, wearing a smile that held absolutely no warmth or kindness. The longer he trained it on me, the further my stomach dropped until it was somewhere around my ankles before he spoke again, his voice filled with a heavier hint of disdain—if that were possible. "Just to let you know, you're not going to score points by showing up this early. You can spare yourself the trouble if you think it's going to get you anywhere."

"Who said I thought it was getting me anywhere?" I asked in genuine confusion. No, this was not the man I remembered from the wedding, but then he had been tipsy, coming off what had to be a long day full of wedding stuff. He wasn't sitting at a desk, absorbed with business. "I'm not interested in scoring points," I assured him, though it was sort of a lie. Showing up early was part of that whole make-yourself-indispensable thing. "I wanted to get a little extra time to settle in on my first full day. That's all."

"Sure. If you say so." Clearly, he didn't believe me.

What had I done that was so wrong? Frustration swelled up in my chest. I never did well with being misunderstood, and this was worse than that. It wasn't that he misunderstood me. He was determined to be a dick, already making up his mind about me and my motives.

What was I supposed to do? Let him sit there and talk to me like that just because of who his father happened to be? Or did he think he was going to get away with it because he was good in bed? If so, he was truly pathetic. Either way, I looked at him with fresh eyes, and I didn't like what I saw. "Mr. Diamond—"

"Really?" he asked, scoffing. "Are we doing that?" God, his sarcasm. And I thought I fell back on it too much. I would have to tell Mom I met somebody who used it even more than I did. She'd be so impressed.

"Lucian," I amended, carefully enunciating through a tight and entirely insincere smile. "Things don't have to be awkward for us just because of what happened."

"Is that what you think? Like I can't handle being in the same room with a woman I was intimate with?" His head snapped back like he was genuinely surprised.

The man was a goddamn enigma, one I wouldn't try to solve if it weren't for my job and everything hanging on it. I should've known better than to think things were going to magically change all because I was making a little more money. My life didn't go that way. It never had.

And that was probably what had me so close to losing my shit as he continued sneering at me from behind his desk. A rush of heat washed over me, settling in my chest. "All I'm saying is, you don't need to worry about me making anything out of it. I'm an adult. It wasn't like we knew we would end up working together."

"Is that the explanation you're going with?" he asked, arching an eyebrow.

"What do you mean?" I fired back.

Lifting a thick shoulder, he muttered, "If it means keeping your job in this tough market? I'm sure you'd say anything."

Something hot and bitter exploded in my chest, sending fire racing through my limbs and making my blood boil. This fucking bully. He might as well have hovered a finger an inch from my face and chanted *I'm not touching you* like some playground menace. I had left those days behind long ago. What a shame I couldn't say the same for him.

"I don't say anything I don't mean, *Lucian,*" I told him, emphasizing his name again. "But if you're going to have a problem treating me professionally, maybe this isn't going to work out."

"Oh, I know it's not going to work out, *Poison* Ivy," he assured me, making my stomach sink further than it already had. He had even given me a nasty nickname! Everything was going wrong, all of it, and all I could do was watch it fall apart.

"I have no choice but to pretend I think otherwise, *Poison,*" he continued. "So please, go out and find your desk, get yourself all settled in like the hard worker you are. You're supposed to be helping me learn the ropes of my new position. Go figure out a way to do that."

What was going to stop me from throwing something at his fucking head? I bit my tongue until it hurt. It was all that got me out of his office before I said something I would definitely get fired for. If it wasn't for Mom, I would've said it, anyway. It would've been worth watching his reaction.

But I couldn't afford to be selfish. Mom had gone through hell to raise me on her own, working nonstop to keep a roof over our heads and food in the kitchen. The least I could do to pay her back would be to put up with an asshole with hands that worked the kind of magic no vibrator had ever managed. How unfortunate, the way my brain insisted on reminding me of that as I walked to my desk on trembling legs.

One thing was for sure. I had worked too hard for too long to let some spoiled rich kid take what was mine. Three years younger than me, with absolutely no experience, and I was supposed to give him a crash course in what I'd learned through years of trial and error. Everything I had, I'd earned, unlike him. For all I knew, that was what he resented. The spoiled brat couldn't imagine earning a damn thing and hated the idea of me being around to keep him on his toes.

And I would.

He could be sure of that.

I sat at the desk in front of his office and set my bag underneath, pulling out my patent leather heels and sliding into them like I'd slide into armor before battle. In a way, that's exactly what I was doing.

He wanted to do things the hard way? Fine by me. I had been playing life on hard mode from the beginning. If anything, he was the one with a lesson to be learned.

I couldn't wait to be the one to teach him what a bad idea it was to play with *Poison* Ivy.

3

LUCIAN

It wasn't a surprise to find Ivy sitting at her desk by the time I arrived at the office for an early breakfast meeting with my father. Our usual Wednesday ritual in the few weeks since the Jones Media buyout was struck, when he had brought me on in an official capacity as opposed to the summers I'd interned here. I was under no illusions—this was not a means of solidifying our relationship or anything like that. He liked to get a look at me and wanted to make sure I wasn't letting my nighttime activities get in the way of what needed to be done during the day.

When exactly did a person become old enough to become a complete hypocrite? It was either that, or he couldn't remember the shit he'd gotten up to in his day. Considering his memory was as sharp as ever, so sharp it made me hate him when he would bring up something I said or did years ago for the sake of winning an argument, I'd have to lean on hypocrisy as the winning theory.

I had asked my mother about it once, around the time I graduated college, and she had laughed it off. It was all part of getting older. Mellowing out, with the memories mellowing too. Like he had never gotten home, showered, then gone to the office without catching a wink of sleep.

In other words, my nerves were already on edge because I knew how closely he would scrutinize me when I reached his office at eight sharp. Finding Ivy bright and chipper, already pounding away on her keyboard when I arrived, didn't make things much better.

Though she was easy on the eyes. Much nicer to look at than my old man. With her shining blonde hair pulled back in a low bun, I admired the graceful lines of her neck. Like a swan. Something that had first caught my attention at the country club before those eyes of hers had pierced me.

And she hadn't known who I was? How was that possible? The only child of a billionaire media mogul. Did she not pay attention to that sort of thing? Granted, I'd managed to keep my name out of the papers and tabloids, if only to keep from getting flayed alive. And she didn't come from my world. Billionaires were probably as familiar to her as long-term relationships were to me. Maybe it was possible… or maybe she would say anything to cover her ass. I couldn't be sure.

She noticed me sizing her up on my way out of my office. Her head turned, her lips curving in a cheerful smile. "Good morning, Mr. Diamond," she chirped. It was almost enough to make me stumble, knocked off-balance by her attitude.

What was she playing at? It wasn't a matter of only being professional. A simple greeting would have covered the bases. No, she had to go above and beyond, swiveling in her chair to follow my progress past her desk.

"Good morning, Poison," I murmured, keeping my voice low in case there was anyone nearby to hear.

Her eyes hardened before she widened her smile until it went brittle. "Is there anything I can do for you this morning? It looks like you have a meeting with your father in a few minutes. Do you need to be prepared?"

I knew how to silence that smart mouth. An image of her on her knees with a mouth full of my cock sprang to mind. "I think I can handle it," I told her, my voice coming out a little gruff.

"You sure?" she asked, head tipping to the side. "I'm only trying to find ways to help you learn the ropes of your new position."

Throwing my words in my face. Wasn't she in a mood today. Only the thought of what she could report back to Dad kept me from telling her to fuck off if she knew what was good for her before continuing past her desk without a word, heading to the opposite corner of the floor, where Dad's office sat. She snorted softly behind me, but I pretended to ignore it, continuing down the hall while reminding myself of my place. She was nothing, nobody. A good lay with a tight pussy. A dime a dozen, in other words.

What a shame she looked so damn good in those suits she wore—slim cut, hugging her every curve. The universe was throwing me a bone, giving me something to look at as I suffered the indignity of some nobody with great tits taunting me from her desk. Not that she had to actively taunt me. Her mere presence was enough to remind me of how I fell short in my father's eyes.

Dad's assistant offered a warm smile as I approached her desk in front of his office. "Good morning, Lucian. Your father is waiting for you." Cynthia had been with Dad for as long as I could remember and was practically a part of the family. She sized me up with a practiced eye as I passed her desk. "Is that a new suit? It's very well-tailored."

"Thank you. Picked it up last week." I checked out the

fresh, colorful bouquet on her desk and arched an eyebrow. "New boyfriend?"

"Now, you know I'm taken," she chided with a soft laugh. "Twenty-two years and counting."

"If only I were a little older..." I sighed, snapping my fingers like I was disappointed. This was our harmless game, reaching back to my interning days. It made Dad grind his teeth, which was a big part of why I continued teasing her—as if I'd end up getting the company sued for harassment or something.

The man had a habit of walking around almost silently. Out of nowhere, he appeared in his open doorway, wearing an exasperated grin. "Could you please stop charming Cynthia so she can get her morning started?" he nearly growled out, waving me into the room.

I looked over my shoulder to where Cynthia's lips twitched as she tried and failed to hold back a grin. "You hear the way he talks to me?" I whispered, and she laughed behind her hand, shaking her head.

Once we were alone, Dad shook his head too. "You seem to be in a pretty good mood this morning," he observed, pressing the button on his desk, which turned the clear glass walls opaque for the sake of privacy. "I take it that means you had a successful evening."

Any goodwill flowing through me died a quick death at the sound of his voice and the disapproval in it. "I had an early evening, now that you mention it." I joined him at the small table in the far corner of the room, where he sometimes took meetings during meal times. Our customary breakfast was spread out and waiting for us. Bagels, cream cheese, and smoked salmon. There was plenty of hot coffee in an insulated carafe, along with orange juice and fresh fruit salad.

"Turning over a new leaf?" Why the hell was there so much enthusiasm in the question? Jesus Christ. He couldn't be more transparent if he tried.

I had no idea what the hell my personal life had to do with him. He hadn't given a shit since I moved into my own Upper West Side apartment when I was nineteen. Why did he care now? Since I wasn't in the mood for an hour-long lecture, I didn't bother asking.

Instead, I settled for shrugging, taking a seat, and pouring coffee. "I'm the lone wolf now," I explained with another shrug.

"You know, I was thinking about that just the other day."

Again, did he have nothing better to think about? "Let me guess," I ventured with a smirk, glancing up at him while smearing a thick layer of cream cheese on a bagel. I didn't eat breakfast often, but when I did, I liked to go all in. "You and Mom had a nice, long discussion about me over a bottle of wine. You've decided now that since my friends have gotten involved and are starting to get married and all that, it's my turn."

"You don't have to sound condescending," he warned, fixing his own bagel.

"It isn't condescension if I'm basing my guess off of reality. Both of you have best friends whose kids just got married last month, and they're going to have a baby. Everybody else is with their significant others now too. Of course, you would start thinking about me."

"You're twenty-five, Lucian."

"So it says on my driver's license," I muttered, taking a bite of a sandwich piled thick with salty salmon.

He groaned, then added, "It's time to start thinking about the life you're going to build."

I lifted an eyebrow. Again, with the hypocrisy. "What

were you doing when you were twenty-five? Because last I checked, you're knocking on sixty now, meaning you had more than your share of fun between twenty-five and when you and Mom settled down together."

"I see. Now you decide what to follow in your father's footsteps. But only in this respect, right?"

I was not interested in getting into it, especially not at this hour of the morning. "Anyway, it's not as much fun to go out by myself with everyone busy all the time..."

"That can only be a good thing," he insisted.

I had to settle for chewing my bagel harder than necessary, gnashing my teeth, swallowing back my true thoughts as I choked down a mouthful of food. "*Your father means well.*" One of Mom's favorite lines. It was only knowing how much it upset her when we fought that kept me from telling him what I thought about his well-intended advice.

I needed to change the subject fast, and only one topic came to mind. "So, tell me. How long is that girl going to shadow me?"

"Ivy? She isn't shadowing you," he scoffed, shaking his head as he wiped his mouth. "I swear, son, you come up with the strangest ideas."

"And you are much too comfortable gaslighting me," I countered. "If she's not shadowing me, what is she here for?"

"You've been steaming over this for two days, haven't you?" He could have at least tried not to seem so pleased at the idea, the old prick. "You have no experience. She is here to help you gain that experience."

"I thought experience was earned over time. Am I missing something?"

"We don't necessarily have that time. We're looking to expand our digital division, and if you're going to spearhead it, you need to hit the ground running. This is no time to doggy paddle and flail your way around."

I had never failed at anything in my life. What I didn't know, I figured out. The word *'can't'* didn't exist. So even though I couldn't have given a wet shit about the company, Dad's legacy, or any of it, I wasn't about to step down if only to prove him wrong about me.

He finished his coffee and set the cup aside with a sigh. "I admit, we haven't had the chance to do much talking about the game plan when it comes to incorporating the new employees into our current framework."

I waved a hand, scoffing. "Why would you want to do that? I'm only your son and a new vice president. Why would you clue me in?"

He narrowed his eyes. "Let's put the hurt feelings aside, shall we? The idea here is to get a sense of how everyone is working together, whether they can be an asset to the company."

There had to be something truly wrong with me since my polluted stream of consciousness immediately connected the word asset to the word 'ass,' which brought Ivy's rather perfect ass to mind. I had no business thinking about her.

"Who said anything about hurt feelings?" I asked, annoyed with myself for letting her distract me again.

"Then, once we're clear on who can best serve us, we trim the fat. Identify redundancies, thank the people we don't need for their service, and we move on stronger than ever. That is the general idea." Narrowing his eyes, he asked, "Are you satisfied? Or is there something you think you could do better?"

It was as if I hadn't spoken. Not that I needed an answer.

My input was never relevant. "So anybody who thinks their job here is set in stone needs to think again," I concluded.

"That is the long and short of it, yes."

"Do they know that?" I asked.

He smirked, chuckling. "And set off a war with people clawing at each other to keep their job? No doubt they know they have to prove themselves. That's enough."

This, I could live with. For the first time in days, hope sparked in my head. "Is Ivy one of the potential redundancies? Since she's only supposed to usher me into my position."

His forehead creased in a familiar scowl. Great. I had pushed too hard and overplayed my hand. I should've known better, but something about her took everything I knew and threw it out the window. She stood in my way, and that was a problem.

"You have a real hard-on for this girl, don't you?" he asked.

What a choice of words. I certainly had a hard-on for her when we first met. "Did you expect me to be happy? You gave me this position, then assigned someone to... what? Micromanage me? Or is this flat-out babysitting?"

"Lucian. Let's get one thing straight." I knew what I was in for when he used those words. He pushed what was left of his breakfast aside, staring at me the way he used to when I would say or do something to irritate him enough to pay attention to something other than this fucking company. "You're a person with many talents. And you know that over the years, I've been disappointed when you haven't used them the way you should. You insult yourself more than you insult me when you ask a question like that. It's childish, beneath you."

"But having her looking over my shoulder isn't supposed to insult me? Explain that, Dad, because I'm at a loss."

"I know you aren't demanding I explain a damn thing to you. Is this or is it not still my company?" He rose, glaring at me the way he had countless times before. "And like it or not, son, you don't have the experience to take a position like this and run with it. Being skilled at using social media for your own personal purposes is not the same as running the digital media division, but I know you can work your way into it. I'm sure you can. It will take time, and you will need guidance."

He shook his head and clicked his tongue, looking as disappointed as he ever had. "There I was, thinking you would understand that without having it spoon-fed to you. For someone who's usually quick on the uptake, you are an expert at playing dumb when you feel like it."

My resentment followed his disdain the way lightning followed thunder. "Sure, accuse me of playing dumb. That's definitely going to make all of this work so much better." I jerked a thumb toward the closed door. "The girl said it herself on Monday. She barely had a chance to make a difference at Jones Media before the buyout. How do you know she has the first idea what she's doing?"

"She may not have been able to turn things around for them, but analytics don't lie. There was a more than three hundred percent improvement in ad revenue month over month in the first quarter of this year. Sadly, it was a little too late. The girl knows what she's doing."

He went to his desk, talking as he walked. "If I remember correctly, she double majored in journalism and digital marketing at Brown on a scholarship, then spent three years managing social media for a handful of small businesses while publishing editorial content to Medium before she took the job with Jones Media."

He pulled a file folder from the deep bottom drawer of his desk and opened it, flipping through then continuing, "She started as a basic advice columnist while working her way up to junior editor over two years. She then pivoted to digital media and did her darndest to convince the owners to move away from print."

Did he expect applause? Was I supposed to be impressed? Okay so maybe I was, but I wouldn't give him the satisfaction. "Good for her," I replied, shrugging.

"Goddammit." He closed the folder before closing his eyes and leaning back in his leather chair. "Put your ego aside and learn something. That's all I ask."

"And all I ask for is a little confidence. Is that too much?" I stood and tossed my napkin onto my half-empty plate. "Are you sure she understands her place in the hierarchy? Or does she think she's here to steal my job?"

He shrugged, the lines at the corners of his eyes deepening when he frowned. "Why don't you see to it she doesn't get the wrong idea? If the position seems vulnerable, easy to steal from under you, that sounds like a *you* problem. Right?"

The miserable old prick. "I hear you." And did I ever.

"Now go out there and learn something," he concluded, waving a hand toward the door. "Prep for your meeting with the team next week. How are you going to bring everybody together? How will you fill any perceived weaknesses with the strengths of our newcomers?"

His questions didn't piss me off. It was the fact that I hadn't considered them before now. Since I had nothing to say, I decided it was smartest to get the fuck out and put together the answers.

Though I'd be damned if I asked Ivy for help. It would be a cold day in hell when I asked her for anything that didn't involve her mouth wrapped around my cock. Since the chances of that happening again were slim to none, thanks to our professional relationship, there was nothing she could do for me but serve as a reminder of how useless my father thought I was.

4

IVY

"So what do we think after our first week?" I looked around the table, taking in the sight of my old coworkers from Jones Media. While we had crossed paths throughout the week, this was the first time we were able to sit down and catch up without any longtime Diamond employees listening in. It wasn't that I was worried about the wrong people overhearing and retaliating but more like nobody felt comfortable opening up and sharing in our new place of business.

But a restaurant offsite? That was a totally different story. All bets were off. Laney Foster, my work bestie, shrugged as she reached for a slice of pizza from the pies sitting in the center of the table. "I mean, it's been fine. One company is the same as another."

"That's not true," Chuck Moran countered. He was around fifty, on the verge of becoming a grandfather in the next couple of months. He took off his glasses and cleaned them on his necktie while wearing a sour expression. "Things aren't the same. I thought the whole point of having lunch together was to feel like we could be honest."

"I was being honest," Laney snapped. The small diamond stud in her nose sparkled when her nostrils flared. "But I'm trying to look at the bright side too. Being negative isn't going to get us anywhere."

"I'm a little worried." Barbara Ross was closing in on retirement age, though I understood too well that certain concepts didn't always apply to everybody equally, like being able to retire just because a certain number of birthdays have been crossed off on the calendar. She couldn't afford it yet and didn't know if she would ever be able to. "I'm at least ten years older than almost everybody else in the company."

"Not true," I pointed out as gently as I could. "I mean, look at Mr. Diamond. He's around your age, right?" Sometimes, it was a little awkward trying to bolster a woman so much older than me, but I had learned over time how to ignore that. It seemed like they had too. Leadership didn't have an age limit.

She gave me one of her wry grins, but it was short-lived. "You know what I mean. The CEO doesn't count."

"What happens when they decide we're too old to fit in?" Chuck asked as he looked around the table. "Upper management can afford to be middle-aged or older. People like us? We're expendable."

"That's age-based discrimination, and it's illegal," Molly Kramer countered, sitting up a little straighter. "Besides, if we do good work, that's all that matters." Chuck's snort and Barbara's eye roll told me what they thought about her trying to look at the positive side of things.

I wished there was something I could say to make things better. The fact was, they had a point. It was one thing for everybody to work together at Jones Media, where the whole concept of everybody being a family and working together was more than simple lip service. After a week with the Diamonds and their extensive staff, I had yet to get a feel for who was safe and who wasn't.

Nobody had to explain it for me to understand. There were bound to be redundancies. Overlaps. Like the overlap between Lucian and me. Did he honestly think his father would choose me over him? Was that where his shitty attitude and dirty looks were coming from? Already, he had pushed me to my limit, and we hadn't come to the official end of the week yet.

"Sometimes I feel like I'm not rich enough to work there," Molly confessed, blushing as she looked around the table. "Does that sound bad?"

"Not at all," I promptly replied since I understood too well what she meant. I had felt that way my entire life in one way or another. At Brown, I was the poor girl trying to fit in, always feeling like a fraud next to everybody else who seemed to naturally understand how to act or be. "But I'm sure it's not true."

"It's a whole new world," Laney pointed out, dipping her crust into a cup of ranch dressing. "There's a lot to get used to. Like, they actually make fresh sushi for lunch. Who does that?"

"I had the most delicious, freshly made waffle yesterday for breakfast," Barbara said with a happy sigh. "That, I could get used to. What a shame I'm afraid to."

"I don't know about any of you, but I'm going to take advantage of that gym." Brad Brooks grinned my way from the other side of the table. Before the Diamond buyout, he had always been the office heartthrob. Barely over thirty, an all-American hunk with the body of a pro athlete, thanks to all the time he spent in the gym. "It's going to save me a hell of a lot of money in fees, and the equipment is top-of-the-line."

"And they cover school costs," I pointed out now that he had gotten me thinking along those lines. "So if anybody wants to go back to school and get their masters, this is the time to do it. I know they offer childcare vouchers too, don't they?" I asked, looking at Molly and thinking of her twin girls.

"That's true. It's a huge help." She pretended to wipe sweat from her forehead. "There are definitely more positives than negatives to the situation. We have a lot to be grateful for."

Still, the energy around the table was a little low as we wrapped up our meal and settled the check. My heart sank at the sight of their worried expressions. There was nothing I could say to ease their worries.

Brad took his time getting up from his seat, and I knew why before our eyes met. There was a time when I had considered going out with him since he had never bothered to hide his interest. For the sake of work, he always kept things professional, but there was something to be said for the lyrics of that old Bonnie Raitt song. He laughed a little too loud and stood a little too close, and right now, he was staring openly, hanging on my every move.

Normally, I was only a little put off by how obvious he acted. I didn't take it personally in a bad way—he was a nice guy, and he never pushed. For some reason, today, of all days, I was not in the mood to perform our little dance.

"You're doing your best," he told me in his usual overly-familiar manner, patting my arm as I slung my purse over my shoulder. "I know everybody appreciates you getting some of us together to check in."

"I wish more of us could get together," I admitted,

politely ignoring the intimacy in his touch. "But I get the feeling we are a pretty decent cross-section of the group as a whole. Everybody's wondering where their place is in the grand scheme of things."

"It's growing pains. They'll get over it." I had never met anyone as confident as him, but was this confidence or arrogance? There was a fine line.

Arrogance naturally brought a certain man to mind as we left the restaurant. I could be blocks away, walking with my friends and trying not to sweat to death, and Lucian managed to take control of my thoughts. He had way too much power over me.

I didn't need to be thinking about him now. What mattered was finding a way to make my people feel more comfortable. As the highest-ranking employee included in the buyout, I sort of felt responsible for them.

Laney must have read my quiet attitude accurately. She knew the odd relationship I had with Brad and how his attention could be equal parts flattering and irritating. That was why she wedged herself between us on the sidewalk and linked an arm around mine, winking at me. "Any plans for the weekend?" she asked, distracting Brad and giving me a little peace. I tuned them out while mulling over the issue at the front of my mind. *Forget Lucian.* My people needed help.

By the time we reached our building and made it to the top floor, my mind was made up. We needed an event. Something small but more relaxed than the *welcome to the family* event we had to sit through on our first day. What a strange experience that had been, but then I was a little too interested in Lucian to pay much attention. I doubted I missed much.

Everybody split up, heading to their desks, while I hesitated near the elevator. Connor's office was clearly visible from where I stood, and it looked like we might have just missed crossing paths with him.

He removed his navy suit jacket and hung it over the back of a chair, then rolled up his shirt sleeves. I might be able to catch him before he got busy.

This would either be a great idea or a grave mistake that left me wishing I was never born. It was too late for second thoughts as I marched across the floor, remembering how sad and scared Barbara was. How nervous Chuck sounded.

Connor's assistant hadn't returned to her desk yet, meaning there was nobody to stop me from approaching the office door and knocking against the glass. This was it. No turning back now. Sometimes, it was a matter of acting before my brain could stop me.

That didn't make it easier to go through with entering the CEO's office once he waved me in, wearing a friendly grin. "Ivy. I'm so glad you caught me. I've been meaning to ask how things are going with Lucian and how the two of you are working together."

We *weren't* working together. That was one of my many problems. While I'd sent him my analytics reports and offered a list of ideas for how to apply my tactics to the current slew of sites owned by the company, Lucian had barely acknowledged my efforts. Should I mention that, or would it come off too whiny? "Things are going well," I lied, taking the safer bet. "I'm looking forward to our first official meeting with the team on Monday. But I had something I wanted to run past you now."

"What can I do for you?"

Good question. So this is how a deer feels when the headlights bear down on them. "I had an idea. You're free to shoot me down, of course." *Great lead-in, genius. He's the fucking CEO. He can tell you to get your shit together and leave too.* "After chatting with some of my coworkers from Jones, I wonder if a small retreat might help them feel like they're gelling with the rest of the company. A way for us to spend time together offsite, to do team building exercises and that sort of thing. I realize it sounds trite—"

"Don't," he warned, shaking his head after cutting me off.

"Pardon?" I squeaked out. *Cool. Now, you sound like a cartoon character.*

"Don't put your own ideas down before you've finished expressing them, and certainly never in the presence of the person you're attempting to convince." He lowered his brow, his mouth twitching into the beginning of a grin. "Got it?"

"Got it. Thank you." He wasn't a bad guy. A little intimidating, but not bad. "I haven't put any actual planning into the idea. It only occurred to me within the last minute or so."

Now he grinned full-out, looking me up and down. "I'm impressed. You have a flash of inspiration and jump into action. Too many people talk themselves out of what might be a genius idea. How many genius ideas never see the light of day?"

"That's a good point." And now I felt much more relaxed. He hadn't agreed, but he hadn't shot me down, either. I decided to take it as a positive sign. "What do you think? It wouldn't have to be anything lavish. We might be able to find space at a hotel somewhere in the area or..." I didn't know what else to say. He made a good point about getting fear out of the way and rushing headfirst into the unknown, but there was something to be said for preparation.

"Say no more. It's a great idea, and I wish I'd thought of

it before you brought it to me." Something behind me caught his eye, he lifted an arm, and waved somebody in. "I want to tell Lucian about this."

Oh, fuck. And I was feeling so positive too. I couldn't exactly ask the man not to include his son in this discussion or else risk questions about a very uncomfortable situation. If it came down between Lucian and me, who would be out on their ass before the end of the day?

Looking over my shoulder, I watched Lucian approach the room. His eyes narrowed a fraction when they landed on me. Would he be immature enough to start trouble in front of his dad? I doubted it. Not in front of Mr. We're All A Big Family Here. Even so, I was guarded, afraid to breathe by the time he entered the office and changed the temperature in the room.

"Was there a meeting nobody told me about?" he asked, his narrowed gaze bouncing between us. No wonder he looked suspicious. God forbid he be left out of something. Was he that insecure about his job?

"Nothing that formal," Connor told him. "Ivy has come up with a great idea to help merge our two factions. What if we hold a retreat? We always have a standing invitation at the lodge up in the Catskills."

"Exactly when do we plan on doing this?" Lucian eyed me and somehow managed to look neutral, except when it came to the thin line his lips pulled into. "It's the middle of the summer. He'll be booked solid up there."

"Let me worry about that," Connor insisted with a gentle laugh. Wealthy people could afford to think that way, like life would gently move aside because they wanted something. He turned to me and explained, "My good friend, Alex Schwartz, owns half a dozen properties up there. If he has to shift a few guests from one to the other for the sake of making room for us, he'll do it. He owes me one."

"And exactly what are we going to do during this retreat?" Lucian had slowly turned my way. It took a lot to bear up under the weight of his stare. "Any thoughts?"

"I'll come up with something," I assured him, extra chipper just to piss him off. I had no idea why it was so important, me getting under his skin, probably because he acted like a spoiled bully, regardless of how good he was in bed. "Team building exercises, that kind of thing. The main idea is to get out of the office, to let us all bond a little more."

"But—" Lucian's mouth snapped shut when his father shot him a sharp look that damn near made me pee myself, and I wasn't the one he was looking at. He could turn the charm on and off with no effort. Whatever silent message passed between them, it was enough for Lucian to nod before speaking. "I'm sure it will be a success. And Ivy," he added, eyes blazing when they locked with mine. "Be sure to let me know if you need any help with the planning. Between this and teaching me how to do my job, I can't imagine where you'll find the time."

"I'm pretty good at multitasking," I offered since I couldn't let him get a dig in without making a dig of my own. "It's how I got where I am." *While all you had to do was be born a Diamond.*

"You can ask Cynthia for help," Connor offered while Lucian's jaw ticked. "We've organized events like this before. She's a genius."

"Thank you. Really, thank you so much for taking my idea seriously." Did I look a little smug when I glanced Lucian's way as I turned to leave the room? Maybe. And maybe he deserved it. It was increasingly obvious he had never met an obstacle that didn't magically get out of the way just because he wanted it to. Poor baby.

Rather than stick around to talk to his dad, he fell in step beside me on my way to my desk. To anyone who might have noticed us, we probably looked completely innocent— two colleagues having a conversation. "Nice move, Poison," he muttered from the corner of his mouth. I didn't know what was more absorbing, the leathery scent of his cologne or the mental image of shoving him into a cubicle.

"I don't know what you're talking about," I whispered while my legs trembled. It wasn't all out of anger, either. When our arms brushed, my stomach flipped. Why couldn't he have been physically repulsive as he was otherwise? It all would have been so much easier to manage.

"Let's get one thing straight. You're not going to score extra points and take control of the digital division by kissing the CEO's ass."

"Now, I'm disappointed." We reached my desk, and I came to a stop, folding my arms as I took in the sight of his stony expression. Dammit, he looked even hotter this way. "I honestly thought you were more mature than this. I'm only looking out for my people."

"Your people?" His eyebrows lifted at my choice of words, and I instantly regretted them. That wasn't the sort of thing I needed to say out loud. "They're *our* people, Poison. Diamond employees. The days of Jones Media are over. You would do well to remember that."

The smugness. That was what took my irritation and pushed it over the top. With my teeth gritted, I replied, "And you would do well to remember I don't report to you, I don't owe you a thing, and I'm doing what I feel is right for the entire company. Maybe you need to think a little more about that and a little less about your pride... Mr. Diamond," I added with a simpering smile. I even batted my eyelashes because why not?

He was practically seething by the time he lifted a finger. "You had better hope this idea of yours doesn't blow up in your face, Poison," he warned.

The problem was I was hoping for the same thing. All I could do was pretend his attitude didn't bother me while I quaked inside. "It won't," I promised with the same wide, insincere smile that so clearly irked him. He scoffed before continuing into his office and turning the glass opaque, effectively blocking himself from my view.

Now, I could let out the breath I was holding when I sank into my chair with a soft groan. All I wanted was to do the right thing for my friends, which somehow made him more determined than ever to view me as an adversary. I couldn't win.

Yes, you can. Hopelessness turned to something fierce and hot, flickering in my chest. I could win by showing him up, making myself indispensable if not to him, then to his dad and the company. The man was making me lose sight of my true goal—keeping this job and keeping Mom safe and cared for.

I would put together the greatest retreat ever, just like I'd work magic with the company's digital division starting with our meeting early next week.

And if I happened to throw Lucian's attitude in his face while I did it? Even better.

5

LUCIAN

"So I come in from lunch, and I find her in Dad's office, going over my head with this stupid idea for a fucking retreat. Because, I don't know, we all have to be one big, happy family or some horseshit." I slammed my glass on the bar after emptying it. "Another, right here!" I shouted to the bartender, who nodded his acknowledgment.

The bar was as busy as usual on a Friday night, which was a shame since I was not in the mood to be patient. What little patience I possessed on a good day had dissolved hours ago.

"Ooh, a corporate retreat." My cousin, Colton Black, winced like he was in pain because that was the effect corporate retreats had on people. Even I knew that, and I'd hardly been part of the corporate world for more than a handful of weeks.

"I have good news for you." Dad's broad smile did nothing to ease the dread that had settled in my bones the second I received his call demanding I come down for a last-minute meeting. How many times had he called me down to his office when there was good news to share? Never. That was how many.

"I can hardly wait to hear it." I didn't bother hiding my disinterest as I flopped into a chair before scrubbing my hands over my face, groaning at the way my head pounded. Of all mornings for him to pull his shit, he would choose the morning after a friend from college threw a divorce party. We had closed down the bar, then the after-hours club we'd moved on to.

Once I lowered my hands, I found Dad scowling. *"If you're feeling under the weather, you should've told me so."*

"I told you I wasn't feeling up to this, and you refused to listen." I barely stifled a yawn for the sake of ending the argument and getting this over with. *"I had a long night. Don't take it personally."*

"At your age, your long nights should be the result of burning the midnight oil. Building something for yourself."

To think, I dragged my ass out of bed for this, being forced to listen to the same hypocritical song I'd heard so many times. *"Can we not do that today? I don't want to hear it. Why did you need me to come in?"*

The second his eyes narrowed, I would've sworn a noose tightened around my neck. *"Since you seem disinterested in working toward something of your own, I'm naming you Vice-President of our growing digital division now that we're absorbing the employees from Jones Media."*

And I thought I felt like hell before. A fist closed around my suddenly icy stomach and squeezed until cold sweat coated the back of my neck. *"You're what?"* I managed to choke out.

He sighed like the very act of explaining himself was beneath him. *"You majored in communications and minored in business administration, yet I haven't seen you do a thing with your education in the past three years. I'm giving you the chance to prove all that tuition money wasn't wasted."*

Like he couldn't afford it. More hypocrisy. My blood started to boil, and I gritted my teeth to contain myself. No wonder he didn't *want to have this conversation somewhere private rather than here at the office. The asshole probably wanted witnesses.*

How the fuck was I supposed to know how to run anything? "I don't want this," *I warned. When was he going to laugh and tell me this was a prank? Why wasn't he laughing? Sitting behind a desk, wearing a suit, playing nice for the sake of politics, talk about a fucking nightmare. I wanted nothing to do with it.*

And he fucking knew that. Hell, I had never made it a secret.

"Remind me when I asked if you want it or not." He pushed the chair away from the desk and stood, glaring at me with the morning sun streaming in behind him. "You're taking this position, and you're going to make something out of yourself. One day, I won't be here to run things. It's well past time for you to claim your birthright and learn what it will take to continue the family legacy."

Miles Young was the newest member of our group. He had come to town to take down his wicked stepfather, Magnus Miller, and was surprised to find the man wasn't so wicked after all.

Having not been raised around the rest of us, meaning he didn't know Dad as well as the others, he could maintain a more positive outlook. "Your dad wants to do what's best for the entire company. And the girl probably wants to make her coworkers feel more comfortable so everybody can work together," he pointed out. "Culture shock is a real thing."

"You seem to have blended in pretty well here in the States," Noah Goldsmith reminded him, referring back to Miles' life in London before moving out here.

"Yeah, but this was hardly my first trip overseas. I came out here for business many times prior to making the final move. I was a fish out of water during those early visits. It was rather pathetic." He snickered, raising his glass. "Of course, I worked my ass off to pretend I felt comfortable."

"Let the girl have her retreat." Evan Anderson could afford to be dismissive. He had always known what he wanted to do with his future—one of the most driven people I've ever met. Valentina made a good match when I looked at it that way. She was just as driven and determined to do exactly what she wanted with her life. Neither of them had ever had to fight to be taken seriously after years of screwing around.

"Sure, she gets her retreat," I grumbled. "Next thing I know, she's got my job."

Colton grunted as if he understood. "So that's what's really getting to you? You have to know you're not in any actual jeopardy." He nudged me when I wouldn't look his way, too busy watching the bartender pour me another whiskey. "You know that, right?"

"I didn't even think you wanted the job," Evan pointed out. "You always said the last thing you wanted was to end up sitting behind a desk like your dad does."

"Does that mean sitting back and letting her walk all over me? She's not going to steal this position," I vowed, taking a gulp of fresh whiskey and relishing the burning sensation spreading through my chest.

Something about the looks they shared told me I wasn't getting through. "What?" I demanded, scowling at them.

"Has she told you she wants your job?" Colton asked, leaning forward so I could see him past the bodies of our friends as we sat in a row along the polished bar.

"Oh, right," I replied, scoffing while the rest of them snickered. "That's something that happens. As if she would walk up to me and announce it."

"I guess I'm asking because you seem so damn sure that's what she's in this for." He lifted a shoulder while the others nodded.

"You don't think it's a little too much of a coincidence? We hooked up at the wedding. Then my company purchased hers."

"All of a sudden, it's his company," Evan joked. His laughter was cut short by my glare. "Sorry. Trying to keep things light."

"Nobody asked you to," I snapped. This was all wrong. They didn't need to put up with me acting like a fucking lunatic over this. I knew damn well I would've busted their balls if the positions were reversed.

But the positions were not reversed. Only I understood what it meant to doubt something I thought was a sure thing. The worst part? Deep down inside, in a place I didn't reveal to anyone, I asked myself which sure thing I was doubtful of. My position with the company or her. Did she want me for myself after the wedding, or was it all an act?

Insecurity was not something I was familiar with, and I hated her for introducing me to it. I hated myself even more for being so fucking weak. I didn't do weakness.

"I say fuck her again," Colton advised with a sage nod. "Make her remember what brought you two together. She'll cave."

They weren't getting it, none of them, probably because I couldn't find a way to express myself clearly. "I don't need her to cave. I need her to get out of my way," I reminded them.

"Why?" Noah laughed. "You said it yourself. Redundancies. You should be more worried about proving you know your shit better than she knows hers. That's the only way you're going to win whatever this is the two of you have going on. Make it so she is totally forgotten and unnecessary."

"That's the way," Miles agreed. "Instead of trying to make her look bad, make yourself look better."

Evan snickered. "Or you could do something to sabotage the retreat," he suggested, chuckling. "Throw her off her game."

"Just when I think we've left playground bullshit behind, he comes up with an idea like that." Noah gave him a friendly shove, which Evan returned.

"I'm just fucking around," Evan insisted, laughing. "Obviously, you know better than to do something like that."

Did I?

I made a big deal of laughing it off the way everybody else did, though my thoughts were another story. Was there a way I could interfere? Nothing extreme, and definitely nothing that would point back at me.

As we were parting ways, Colton pulled me aside. "Listen. You have nothing to worry about. Learn what you can from this girl, okay? Your dad is like mine, and he wants the company to be in good hands. He won't drop you to keep her on the payroll. Trust me."

Trust him. Easy to say.

It was Noah's advice that bounced around inside my skull as I stepped out of the bar and into a muggy night. The sidewalks were cramped, and the air reeked of cologne, perfume, and sweat, but not much of it registered on my awareness as I cut through the crowd and climbed into the back seat of my town car. I didn't normally use my driver on an average Friday night, but I'd expected to be blackout drunk by the time we wrapped things up. Unlike my friends, I didn't consider a last-minute Uber a viable option.

I was entirely too sober by the time I settled in against the supple leather. "Where to?" the driver asked from behind the wheel.

If I were going to make Ivy look obsolete, I had to outsmart her. That meant bringing home the files and analytics reports I left on my desk before heading to the bar. "The office," I decided. The last thing I felt like doing over the weekend or, frankly, ever, was analyzing reports.

Desperate times called for desperate measures, such as taking the elevator up to the top floor once we arrived. There was something almost eerie about the profound quiet once the doors opened onto an empty reception desk. It wasn't silence, exactly. The low hum of vacuums and rustling of waste baskets prevented that. Still, it was a far cry from the usual noise audible during the workday.

I laughed off the impulse to walk quietly, slowly, like this was some sacred space I didn't want to disturb. Too many of my thoughts lately were childish ones like that. I had to move past the way Ivy set my teeth on the edge. Colton was right, even if his big cousin bullshit tended to get on my nerves. We weren't kids anymore. I didn't look at him adoringly just because he was a few years older than me.

Once I rounded the corner past the bank of elevators, I stopped short at the sight of a familiar blonde head. She had to be kidding, right? A check of my watch confirmed it was well past eight o'clock and on a Friday, no less. Who the hell stuck around this late on a Friday night?

She cradled the phone receiver between her ear and her shoulder and was so absorbed in her conversation that she didn't notice my slow approach. "I'm sorry, I couldn't make it over tonight. I know. I'm trying." She spoke loudly enough that I heard her plainly, and her obvious strain shone through. This wasn't a side of her she had ever revealed during our interactions. "Remember what I told you. Everything hinges on this. It's important to both of us."

Something hot and bitter raced through me when she

said it. Did she have a boyfriend? And why would it matter if she did? Why was there a burning sensation in my chest now that I'd heard her speak those words?

She caught me out of the corner of her eye, and all at once, a change came over her. Her posture improved, and her tone brightened. "I'll give you a call in the morning, all right? I love you."

I love you...

What the fuck was it about her that turned me into this unrecognizable version of myself? There I stood, biting my tongue when the impulse to ask who she was talking to almost became reality.

"Good evening," she murmured once she'd set the receiver in its cradle. "I didn't expect to see you again until Monday."

"Sorry to disappoint you, Poison," I offered, making her frown. Sure, let her pretend to take the high ground. Let her pretend she had no idea why I would have animosity against her. "I left something in my office."

Why did she have to stare at me that way? With those big, shining eyes that tried to convince me it would be a good idea to make things right with her somehow. To start from scratch and work as a team.

I knew damn well where that would get me. Out on my ass, a confirmed loser who couldn't hack it in a company run by his father. No, thanks. This was the enemy. She didn't need or deserve my empathy.

"Don't let me stop you," she finally muttered, her eyes shifting to the right and landing on my office door. "I'm sure you have better things to do than hang out here."

"You don't?" *Just go, you fucking idiot.* Why would I do things the smart way?

One of her delicate brows arched. "Sure, but I have a ton

to do between getting ready for Monday's meeting and prepping for the retreat."

"Don't blame anybody but yourself for that one."

"I'm not interested in blaming anybody for anything. I was glad my idea was approved. That's all that matters."

"Of course," I offered with a smirk. "Because you're so altruistic."

"Wow. I have to admit, I'm impressed. That's a pretty big word." She leaned back in her chair and folded her arms, and I'd be damned if some perverse part of me didn't warm in anticipation. I wanted a fight. I craved it. What the hell did that say about me?

"Last I checked, you like when I use big things, Poison. Words, my hands, other parts of my anatomy..." I trailed off, grinning when she blushed to the roots of her hair.

"Could you not be so unprofessional?" she hissed. "We both know that was then, and this is now. You don't have to throw it in my face."

"What are you so afraid of?" I challenged, egged on by the way her shoulders crept up around her ears. "We're alone. You don't have to pretend."

"Who's pretending?" She pushed back from the desk, wearing the irritating smile she put on at moments like this. "I'm not interested in rehashing the past. What matters is the work I'm doing now, which was going well until you showed up. Now you've completely destroyed my flow, so I'm going to go home and continue there."

"Are you sure you aren't in a hurry to meet your boyfriend?" I nodded to the phone on her desk. "Let me guess. He doesn't like you working late."

"Wow. When you're off, you're off by a mile." Instead of explaining what that meant, she laughed softly, pulling her leather shoulder bag from the deep drawer under her desk.

I tried not to ogle her ass when she bent over, but I wasn't successful. She was right there, in front of me, practically begging to be touched in the tight skirt, molding itself to her curves. And I knew just how she liked it, whether she pretended otherwise or not.

"So you weren't sitting here asking some guy to understand why you couldn't meet up tonight? I know what I heard."

"What you overheard," she amended, rolling her eyes. "And, of course, that's where your mind went because you probably never had to split your time between work and a sick relative. I was talking to my mother," she explained in an almost ominously quiet voice. "She's been in a nursing home for the past eight months after having a stroke. She needs nursing care much more than anything I could provide on my own, and I'm all she has in the world. I was supposed to visit tonight, but I got too caught up in what I was working on to make it during visiting hours." She pulled back her shoulders and lifted her chin, giving me a superior stare. "Is there anything else you would like to know, or can I go now?"

Fuck me. I could count on one hand the number of times I had felt so intensely like a dick. "I wasn't aware of that," I admitted. My opinion of her softened a little before I could help it. What would it be like, balancing a job like hers with a sick parent and nobody else to fall back on?

"No shit," she muttered, rolling her eyes. "I'm just saying, maybe you shouldn't make assumptions, Lucian."

"Oh? I thought I was Mr. Diamond."

"During working hours," she snapped back, then glanced at her phone. "And we are well beyond working hours. Now, if you'll excuse me, I would like to get home."

I must not have moved fast enough for her. She brushed

against me on her way around the desk and wobbled a little as if I knocked her off balance. Without thinking, I reached out and took her arm, the breath catching in my throat when a chill ran through me.

She looked down at my hand and then met my gaze. Fuck, why did it have to be this way? Everything came rushing back in full color. Her moans echoed in my ears, and the memory of her ambrosial sweetness danced across my tongue. I didn't know women like her existed in real life until the night we spent together. A night I would gladly have relived even now.

To hell with right and wrong. To hell with my pride. I wanted to have this woman again and couldn't pretend otherwise.

"Lucian," she warned, eyes darting back and forth. "There are people here. This isn't right." Her words held no conviction, and the desire burning behind her beautiful orbs told me she wanted this just as much as me.

"What isn't?" I pulled her closer, soaking in her warmth after being without it for so goddamn long. Hating who she was didn't seem to make a difference when it came to loving the way her pussy gripped my cock.

"This. You know what I mean." So what was with the soft gasp when I backed her against her desk? When I lowered my head, inhaling the vanilla citrusy scent of her perfume. She shivered but didn't resist.

The cleaning staff was on the other side of the floor. I could barely hear the vacuums from back here. Nobody saw me brush my lips over the seashell curve of her ear. "You are much too tense, Poison. Let me help you with that. You know how good it is when I do."

"Which is it?" Her breath was hot against my neck

before her lips grazed my scruff-covered jaw. "You want me, or you hate me? It can't go both ways."

"Who says?" I looked her in the eye, barely able to breathe, when I found the same deep, blazing passion that had haunted my dreams for weeks. My dick was hard as steel, and every instinct demanded I take her to my office and bend her over the desk.

"Me." Blazing passion turned to something sharp and cold before she gave her arm a yank, freeing it from my grip. "You need to make up your mind."

This time, I didn't bother trying to stop her. She wanted to go? She could be my guest. If anything, she did me a favor. A few drinks, and I'd fuck damn near anything, apparently. Including the woman working her ass off to unseat me. No one could convince me otherwise. How could I have lost sight of that?

Oh, right. I was horny as hell, and she was the most memorable fuck of my life. My dick was still painfully hard as I watched her walk away, swinging her hips with every quick step. Eager to get home and work on her presentation at a meeting I was supposed to lead. But not so eager that she glanced back at me, her cheeks tinged pink. Our eyes collided before she snapped her head back round.

I had a long weekend ahead of me, but the work would pay off when I crushed this meeting and Ivy's hopes along with it. Sick mom or not, she needed to learn once and for all who she was up against.

6

IVY

In the history of Mondays, this had to be the Mondayest Monday of them all. It wasn't bad enough I had a huge meeting scheduled for nine o'clock on the dot or that my stomach was in knots at the idea of Lucian being there with me, hovering, reminding me simply by breathing how good we were together under different circumstances.

My mother had to fall while insisting on getting out of bed on her own. She couldn't bother waiting for one of the aides to assist her, God forbid. Now she was having x-rays taken, and I could only cross my fingers and pray she hadn't broken anything.

"Please, keep me posted on her progress," I urged the nurse who I'd called for an update before heading into work, where I might not be so easy to reach right away.

I had woken up to multiple messages from the nurses' station asking me to call them back. Usually, they didn't call so many times in a row, and if there wasn't a problem, they would make a point of saying that so nobody freaked out.

When I realized they hadn't, my blood pressure immediately skyrocketed, and I had been on the phone most of the morning by the time I rushed into the spacious lobby, praying I could pull it together in time for the meeting to start in a few minutes. Dammit, I wanted to be early today too.

There hadn't been enough time to be careful with my hair and makeup as I'd wanted to. I looked professional but not well put together. My reflection in the elevator's mirrored doors revealed a wide-eyed woman whose hair looked limp, whose normally fair skin was flushed like a tomato. I ran my fingers through my light blonde locks before searching for a clip in my bag, cursing the cruelty of fate. Today of all days.

For some reason, presenting a solid image meant everything today. Who was I kidding? I knew exactly why, and his name was Lucian Diamond. It was bad enough that I'd thought about him all weekend after he pinned me against the desk Friday night. He always found a way to throw me off with his little quips and reminders of how we first met. I couldn't let him think it was that easy to knock me off balance, even if it totally was.

The list of things I wanted to do before the meeting started was running through my head as I quickstepped my way out of the elevator and down the hall. That list came to a stop when I approached the conference room and found it already full of people. I immediately recognized them as members of my team. Considering they were already chatting and reading something off the screen against the far wall, I could only conclude they started without me. Were we a team, after all?

Instead of going straight to my desk as I had planned, I opened the conference room door and did everything I could not to demand answers. "Hi," I offered, looking around the room. "Did I miss something? I thought we were supposed to get together at nine."

Lucian sat at the head of the table, every inch the imposing businessman in his charcoal suit and crisp white shirt. At any other time, I might have considered eating him up with a spoon, looking as delicious as he did.

This was not any other time. I would gladly have used that spoon to carve his eyeballs from his skull because the bastard had obviously sabotaged me. Was he that much of a bitch? Getting back at me for turning him down on Friday night?

"I'm so sorry. Did you not get the memo?" he asked. The son of a bitch had the nerve to tip his head to the side and frown like he was genuinely sorry, which something told me he wasn't. Maybe it was the way he was trying not to grin while everybody else had their eyes on me. "We had to roll the meeting back half an hour thanks to a conflict with my schedule. Last-minute drama," he added, shrugging like it was just one of those things and hadn't deliberately changed the time without telling me.

Even though my insides were boiling, I couldn't show it. And he knew that. "These things happen," I said with a sigh as I rounded the table, coming to a stop beside Lucian's chair. There was no empty chair for me. Another power play. That was all he had to go on.

Tricks and games.

"Here." Brad, always a gentleman, got up and gave me his chair. I set it down next to Lucian's at the head of the table while Brad grabbed a chair from the corner for himself. From the corner of my eye, I caught a glimpse of the way Lucian glared at him.

Did he know he was doing it? Did he know everybody could see?

"So," I said with a smile, looking around the table. "What did I miss?"

Laney cleared her throat, and the guilty look she wore got me thinking she felt bad for the way things were going. Granted, it's not like she could have made a difference by texting me. I wouldn't have gotten here any sooner. No doubt she figured I'd gotten the same alert she had and knew about the change in schedule. "We were discussing various markets and where we should focus on strengthening our presence."

"I see." I grabbed a copy of the meeting agenda left on the table and skimmed it quickly. Somebody was a busy boy this weekend. As much as it irked me to know how important it was to him to make me look like an asshole, I did get a little rush of satisfaction when I imagined him burning the midnight oil, trying to make himself seem like a legitimate leader.

Looking away from the notes, I asked him, "And you managed to handle everything in my absence?"

The blank shock that passed over his face quickly vanished, replaced by something harder. "We proceeded with the meeting as planned."

"But this must be the first meeting you've ever led," I offered with the wide, insincere smile that so clearly set his teeth on edge. It was wrong of me to get such a charge from pissing him off, but it felt too good. So much so, I couldn't stop, especially considering he tried to sabotage me this morning. "That's a big deal. I remember the first meeting I ever had to take charge of."

Before he could respond, I turned my attention to the rest of the room. "Thank you so much for your patience, and I'm sorry for the miscommunication. Let's pick up where we left off. I would like to hear more about these underserved markets. I've already identified a couple on my own, and it would be nice to see what others have identified."

"Let me bring you up to speed here. We already know that the Midwest and Southwest are the two we're most interested in expanding deeper into, ideally through our digital platform." Lucian tapped his pen against his copy of the agenda, quirking an eyebrow at me. "Do you approve?"

Games.

"Of course," I insisted. If I kept smiling like this, my face would cramp up. "I was thinking along exactly those lines. I pieced together a short presentation, in fact."

"I'm sure we would all love to see it. Maybe you can send it to us to view at our desks later on." He made a big deal of checking his watch before grimacing. "I'm afraid we don't have enough time to set things up now. This was only slated to be a forty-five-minute meeting, and there are still other items we need to address on the agenda."

I was pretty sure I heard Laney sucking in a breath through her teeth. Good. I wasn't the only one who saw straight through his bullshit. It was obvious he was doing everything he could to push me aside. "I would be happy to email it to the team," I offered.

I was proud of myself for getting through this without punching him straight in the face. Why was he doing it? Was he so insecure? From where I was sitting, he had absolutely no reason to be. He was the crown prince, the only child of Connor Diamond. Fate had smiled on him before he was born. If I were anywhere near as lucky as him, I would've spent a good part of every day thanking my lucky stars instead of coming up with ways to squeeze everybody else out.

"I remember some of the ideas you were putting together back at Jones." Laney was doing her best to help me pull things together, and I wished I knew how to feel about it. She was a good and supportive friend, but I didn't need Lucian thinking I couldn't fight my own battles. It wasn't like I could come out and say that kind of thing in front of everybody, obviously, meaning I could only bite my tongue.

"Didn't you already have a plan put together for the Midwest market?" Brad asked.

"Really?" Lucian dragged out the word, swiveling my way. "Maybe that's something you should share with everybody too. I know I would love to hear about it. Unless it was something you were working on privately."

More Games.

This was not a conversation we needed to have in front of the rest of the team. There were more than a few soft coughs, the sound of a few people shifting their weight in their chairs.

"These are only ideas I was working on before I had the pleasure of coming to work here." And what a pleasure it had been so far. If I made it through the rest of this joke of a meeting without murdering him, I would deserve an award.

To think, I had such high hopes. I should've known better. Feeling sorry for myself wasn't something I considered a habit, but I was starting to understand how some people made it their life's mission. All I wanted to do by the time everybody started getting their things together was fold my arms on the table and bury my face in them.

Brad lingered on the other side of the room, looking at me rather than leaving with everybody else. I offered a brief smile and shook my head just enough for him to see and understand.

"Did you need something?" Lucian hadn't gotten his things together, no surprise, and now, point-blank leveled

Brad with a cold stare. It wasn't enough for him to make me look like an asshole in front of everybody. He had to stick around so he could gloat in private. While I didn't want to give him the satisfaction, I had more than a few things I needed to get off my chest.

Brad scowled but left the room, letting the door swing shut behind him. That was as long as it took for me to shove my chair back from the table with a grunt and jump to my feet. "What the hell was that about?" I whispered fiercely, aware of the people sitting only a few yards from where I stood.

The man had the art of looking innocent down pat. "I don't know what you're talking about, Poison," he had the nerve to say.

"Bullshit. You changed the time without telling me." Pulling out my phone, I opened my calendar. "Look. No update, no reminder, nothing. You deliberately kept me out of it for thirty minutes, and for what? To prove you're a big man?"

"I really don't know what you're talking about." He closed his MacBook and even had the nerve to sigh as he stood. "I'm good at a lot of things, as you know, but I don't consider myself a tech genius, so I have no idea why you didn't get an alert about the new meeting time. I look forward to seeing your presentation or whatever it was you put together." If he'd made air quotes around the word presentation, he couldn't have been more condescending.

There wasn't much I hated more than being patronized. Something about it made me see red and always had. My chest painfully tightened as I spat, "You can't handle me being here. Just admit it already."

He clenched his infuriatingly sharp jaw and narrowed his unfathomably dark eyes. Of all times for me to be this aware of how good he looked. "Yes, that's right," he muttered, scoffing. "Keep imagining I care that much about you."

"It's the truth. You can't handle knowing somebody might know more than you do about anything. And what's worse," I added, even as my good sense told me to stop. "You can't handle the idea of there being competition for your position. Welcome to the real world, buddy. That's how it is for everybody."

He had the nerve to lift his chin like he was proud. "I'm not everybody."

"Thank God for that because I don't know how the world would keep spinning if everybody was like you." Boy, was this going off the rails. He had my blood up. I couldn't let him get away with the things he was saying and doing. Somebody had to hold this brat accountable.

"I'm sure it wouldn't be able to keep spinning without people like you." Sneering, he shook his head. "Willing to do anything to get an edge on the competition, even if it means fucking the boss."

At first, I didn't understand what he meant. When he said *boss*, my mind immediately went to Connor, who I, of course, hadn't slept with. Then I remembered being in Connor's office last week and how suspicious Lucian had looked. Is that what he thinks happened before he came in?

It only took a second for my brain to catch up. He was talking about himself. He was accusing me of sleeping with him to get this job and keep it secure. Just when I thought he had scraped the bottom of the barrel, he found a way to go lower.

I didn't know whether to laugh myself sick or cry over how pathetic he was. "You are unbelievable," I said, shaking my head. "You honestly thought that's what this was all about? Like I'm so damn desperate, I would sleep with you to keep my job secure? What is it like living in your head?"

"Sure, give me all the stupid bullshit you want," he insisted. "Don't act like you're above that kind of thing. You would be the only person who refused to use what they had going for them."

"That's usually the case if the person in question has nothing else going for them but what they can do in bed." I could not believe we were having this discussion right here in the office, no less. But at least I now had a clue where his animosity was coming from. Here I was, figuring it all had to do with stepping on his toes in front of his dad. But really, he felt used. Poor little thing. "I have a brain going for me too. Or do you think I fucked my way to where I was at Jones Media?"

I knew it was a mistake before his head snapped back. The last syllable was barely out of my mouth, and I knew I shouldn't have said it. Not here, in the conference room, where we were supposed to at least pretend to be professional.

This is it. You just doomed yourself, your mom, and your whole future.

When his eyes went narrow, I realized I was in a cage with a tiger staring me down. I couldn't exactly run screaming from the conference room, so there was nothing to do but stand straight and tall under his heavy stare. "Let's get one thing straight, Poison," he growled out. "We had fun, but that doesn't give you the right to talk to me the way you do. I am your superior."

"What you are is out of your mind. I actually feel sorry for you right now." I finished getting my stuff together, shaking with rage. More than that. It was the bitter sense of being deliberately misunderstood. Underestimated. No matter what I said, he was going to believe exactly what he wanted because, in his head, that was the way things made sense.

Still, I couldn't help setting him straight on something, turning toward him with my hand on the doorknob. "Let's get one thing straight. You can't live in New York without knowing the name Diamond. I recognized it during the wedding."

"I knew it," he gritted out.

"*But,*" I bit out. "You weren't working here at that time, genius. The press release announcing your appointment as vice president didn't come out for another week, remember? And the only reason I was paying attention to that was we had just heard the buyout was definitely going through. I didn't know you had anything to do with it at the wedding, and I sure as hell didn't know I'd end up holding the hand of a manchild three years younger than me while he got his feet wet in the real world."

I was trembling but somehow managed to hold myself together as I lifted my chin and took in his slightly open mouth and wide eyes. He wasn't expecting that. "Now that I've wasted more than enough time explaining myself to you," I concluded as I pulled the door open. "I'm going to get some actual work done, and not because I want to make somebody else look bad. I actually care about the success of this division."

I'd gotten the last word, which was a victory in and of itself. Why didn't I feel victorious as I hurried to my desk, blinded by the tears I frantically tried to blink back? I ended up ducking into the ladies' room, instead, hiding from the world in the stall at the far end of the row and crying with one hand clamped over my mouth to muffle the sound.

Everything I had worked for was slipping through my

fingers, no matter how hard I tried to hold on. And there was nothing I could do but sit back and let it happen.

Was that true, though?

Once the first wave of emotion passed, I blew my nose and dabbed my eyes. What was I thinking? I wasn't a victim. Okay, so I needed a moment to collect myself. There was no crime in that. Better to weep in a bathroom stall than unleash hell on somebody who was supposed to be my boss. Some little pissant with a trust fund who couldn't for the life of him handle anybody knowing more than he did.

Still, there were ways for me to come out on top. All at once, I went from quietly weeping to smiling when I imagined how it would get under his skin. My body hummed with renewed energy by the time I left the stall to splash my face and freshen up my makeup.

It was almost a shame to find Lucian away from his desk when I reached mine. Maybe he did have another meeting, or maybe he knew better than to show his face after saying he did. Either way, it didn't matter.

I sat at my desk, opened my MacBook, and typed out an email to the digital team.

To: Digital Team – All
CC: Connor Diamond
Re: Meeting Outcomes

Thank you all so much for such a successful first meeting. As we discussed, I have attached a rundown of the underserved markets where our influence could be asserted, along with plans for how to move forward. I would love to circle back on this as soon as possible, and I'm more than happy to answer any questions you might have.

Thank you again, everyone.
Kind Regards,
Ivy St. James

. . .

AFTER ATTACHING the file I was referring to, I made one last tweak. I cc'd Connor. Now, it looked like I had run the meeting and was following up with valuable information that I naturally wanted to share with the company's CEO.

And Lucian would look like a nobody, someone who sat back and let the expert do all the talking.

He wanted to act like a nasty little shit? I could play that game too. At this rate, I had no choice. Not with Mom in such a bad condition, needing more care all the time.

Though I couldn't tell myself I was doing it all for her. Not when a rush of pure satisfaction washed over me after I hit send on the email and imagined what Lucian's reaction would be.

7

LUCIAN

If things kept up the way they were, I'd have to send a company-wide memo. Yes, we knew there was a retreat on the horizon, but work still needed to be done. After hearing about nothing else for the past week since we made the announcement, I was ready to fire the next motherfucker I overheard talking about the lodge or who they hoped their room would be close to. Like this was summer camp and we were all a bunch of kids. Did these people have nothing better to think about? Were their lives that empty?

I passed the break room, where a cluster of women went on and on about what they wanted to bring and whether it would be enough for a weekend. Did they never go away on trips?

"It would've been nice to get a little more warning," one of the women added. Obviously, none of them noticed me lingering near the doorway. "I had to scramble to find a sitter for the kids."

That was something she hadn't considered when she came up with this idea. The thought made me smile to myself as I continued to my office, ignoring the excited chatter. Her desk was empty—no doubt she was checking in with Cynthia, making sure she'd considered every factor. Cynthia had been planning pointless wastes of time like this retreat for years and had it down to a science.

I had done most of my communicating with Ivy via email in the five days since our meeting, and that was much more her doing than mine. The coward could hardly face me. Funny how she started this wanting to play nice and be professional, then turned around and cc'd my father on an email that had nothing to do with him so she could kiss his ass.

It was almost enough to make me double back and tell those harpies in the break room if they had trouble getting childcare lined up, they could thank Ivy for it. She would find out what happened to people who went over my head to make me look like shit.

You started it. Like I needed my inner voice's reminder. When I'd looked back over the timeline of events—the wedding, Dad's job offer that was more of a demand, the press release and buyout finalization—it was perfectly believable that she hadn't known we'd be working together. Would she have fucked me in hopes of getting close to the CEO? When I checked in with myself and looked at the situation honestly, I couldn't believe it. She hadn't made any effort to stay in touch, for one thing. What good would one isolated night have done for her career?

Had all of this been for nothing? A waste of time getting back at her for something that was only in my head?

It was a relief to close my office door and shut out the incessant chatter. We were scheduled to get on chartered buses outside at three, meaning I had a few hours to go until the fun truly started.

This retreat was going to go well in the end. There wasn't a doubt in my mind that Ivy would be incredible at organizing everything, which would earn her even greater approval from Dad.

And make me less likely to keep this goddamn job once he decided she was better suited than me. She already had me looking like an asshole with the presentation she hadn't bothered bringing to me before announcing it to the entire team. There had to be something I could do to pay her back for that little email trick, but what? Short of canceling our reservations at the lodge.

Our reservations.

An idea played out in my mind's eye, so sharp and clear it was like I was watching a movie. One more time, just once, to teach her a lesson. Then we'd be even.

I crossed the room before I could talk myself out of it while pulling out my cell. It took no time to find a number for the lodge, where a chipper young woman was on front desk duty. "Hello," I replied after she answered. "I'm part of the Diamond Media retreat you're hosting this weekend."

"Of course," she chirped. "We're looking forward to your group's arrival later today. I trust everything is going according to schedule?"

"It's funny you should put it that way because we do have a slight problem. Nothing serious," I assured her while gazing out beyond my office walls to the buzzing hive of activity. "But a handful of our people weren't able to secure childcare this weekend and won't be able to join us. Since I know it already had to put you guys out, shuffling things around to make room for us, I thought I should let you know we won't need as many rooms as we originally imagined."

"That is helpful," she agreed. "We currently have sixty rooms booked. How many can we release?"

"Ten," I ventured. "Thank you so much for being willing to work with us on this."

"It's our pleasure. We'll see you all in a matter of hours."

I assured her she would before ending the call and was barely able to stop laughing once I did. No, it wouldn't be enough to shut the entire event down, but it would mean scrambling to make things work. "Let's see how calm you can be under pressure," I murmured, my smile widening when I imagined how flustered she would be.

All of a sudden, I was starting to look forward to this retreat.

∼

There was nothing like the month of July when it came to sudden, violent storms. The sky had threatened all day to open up and drench us. By the time we reached the on-ramp for Route 28, that threat turned into reality. Suddenly, we slowed to a crawl as rain lashed the windows and reduced visibility. As if I wanted to be on a fucking bus any longer than I needed to.

A two-hour drive turned into a four-hour ordeal thanks to an accident on the road ahead, which left us sitting still for much too long. *Thank God for AirPods*, I thought while turning up the volume on the music coming from my phone to block out my surroundings.

Ivy wanted to be a leader? She could lead us out of this.

At least a lot of the noise quieted once the lodge came into view and stunned most of the group into silence. I could admit it was impressive, sprawling upward and outward with multiple peaked roofs, which, from a distance, seemed to compete with the peaks behind them. Like a rustic cabin on steroids.

The lingering rain made me glad of the awning which spanned the entire walkway leading up to the lodge's heavy doors. "Welcome, welcome," the staff murmured like a bunch of robots, standing in a line stretching almost from the front door to the front desk. Clearly, our arrival meant something. I could tell from the awkward stares and soft giggles from more than one of our employees that they weren't used to this level of attention. That didn't come as any surprise.

It also didn't come as a surprise when I found icy blonde hair shining at the front desk as we filtered into the lobby. I crept closer, listening hard but pretending to be clueless. "I don't understand," I heard Ivy say in a tight, slightly panicked voice. "I confirmed the number of rooms with you on Wednesday. I have the email confirming this."

"Yes, but someone called and told us to reduce the number of rooms because there were a number of your group who were unable to make it."

"Someone... called you?" she asked the clerk in a softer voice.

"Yes. Earlier today."

I watched from behind as her shoulders rolled back and her spine stiffened. "I see. There's a ten-room difference, yes?"

"That's right. I'm so sorry."

"Don't worry about it. Really." Ivy certainly sounded worried, though. I hesitated a few moments, letting her stew, always intending to save the day by offering to speak to Mr. Schwartz myself. He would be more than happy to help iron out any issues we had. Maybe I had taken this too far. I'd always planned to fix things, no harm done, but she had the same worry on her pretty face I'd seen before. I now remembered her sick mother Ivy told me about and wondered how much adversity the girl could handle.

"You know, Mr. Schwartz is a personal friend of my family," I offered, coming to a stop at her side. "I could talk with him, arrange for a few of our people to stay at a neighboring lodge. We could shuttle them over here during the day and back at night."

"Unfortunately, we are fully booked in our other lodges," the girl behind the desk told me. "It's our busy season. Plus, we just got word the storm knocked out power in town, so any of the smaller places down there will probably be scrambling around, trying to make do until the lines are repaired."

Fuck me. I didn't count on that. In all honesty, I hadn't given my plan much thought beyond fixing things at the last moment just to prove I could. I hadn't considered violent storms and power outages.

"Do you have cots?" Ivy asked. I craned my neck, hoping to catch her eye, but she pointedly refused to look my way. "I'm sure there have to be a few people who would be glad to double up."

"Yes, we can provide cots to anyone who would be willing to share a room." The look of relief on the girl's face was matched by the sound of it in Ivy's voice when she offered her thanks.

When the clerk hurried off to locate the cots, I opened my mouth, prepared to offer insincere congratulations on saving the day yet again. Her stony stare told me that would not be a wise course of action, putting it mildly. "Don't even start with me," she warned in a whisper. "And don't pretend it wasn't you who did this."

She wasn't an idiot, so her accusation came as no

surprise. Not that it made a difference. "I was about to offer my appreciation for coming up with a solution."

"Bullshit." Just as suddenly as her face had twisted into a snarl, it shifted into an easy-going smile. She waved her arm over her head, and she turned to the group. "Hi, everybody. We're going to need to work together on this."

When a low roar of concerned voices drowned her out, I put two fingers in my mouth and blew out a sharp whistle that silenced the group. Ivy offered no acknowledgment, clearing her throat. "We've hit a little bit of a snag, but it shouldn't be too much of a problem. Through some sort of scheduling mishap, we're ten rooms short this weekend. But they do have cots available for us to use, or maybe those of us willing to share a bigger bed with a friend could help too." Right away, her friend Laney stood up straighter and nodded. She was cute in an offbeat kind of way, but not my type.

"I can stay with Laney!" An older woman—Barbara something—linked arms with the girl in question. "That is if you don't mind. I can always use a cot," she offered. Laney's strained smile and Ivy's disappointed sigh told me what they thought of the arrangement, but neither of them wanted to be rude and tell the woman her help was not helpful at all.

"Thank you, Barbara," Ivy called out. She was masterful when it came to being two-faced, lying to these people to make them feel better. Was that what I had to look forward to for the rest of my corporate life? Playing nice? I couldn't think of many things I would like less.

Eventually, those who were able to pair off did so, collecting their key cards at the front desk before taking a map of the lodge that would direct them to their rooms. The place was so huge I thought it was a castle when Mom and

Dad first brought me here. I wasn't tall enough to see over the front counter then.

Finally, there was no one left but Ivy and me. I wasn't about to let her take charge without at least showing my face and reminding people who I was. Since Dad didn't see fit to join us—not that I could blame him—I had to represent the family. How would he have reacted at the sight of only one room key left waiting on the desk?

"Has there been a mistake?" I asked as evenly as I could, eyeing the card. "There are two of us left, but only one key card."

"That's because there's only one room left, genius," Ivy muttered, snatching the card. "Congratulations. You've given us no choice but to share a goddamn room all weekend."

"That's not happening, Poison," I replied with a laugh. "And save your accusations."

"Sure. This is all a big *coincidence*. The fact that we lost ten rooms and the fact that you hate me for working at your company are completely unrelated." She rolled her eyes, blowing out an exasperated sigh. "I guess I could stay with Laney and Barbara..." Her voice was flat, almost weak. Obviously, the idea didn't make her happy.

But did staying with me? I couldn't imagine it. Yet there she was, hustling quickly across the rustic lobby, holding my room key hostage as she did. "You're sure there are no other rooms available?" I asked the clerk. What was I supposed to do otherwise? Stay with some random employee? Yeah, right.

"I'm afraid not. Sorry." She grimaced like she was sympathetic but did nothing to help.

I had fucked myself royally. What was worse, Ivy knew it. I had no choice but to catch up to her.

"Can I at least get the duplicate key?" I asked, falling in step with her. "Or are you going to keep that from me?"

"As far as I'm concerned, you can go outside, look up at the sky, and open your mouth wide. Maybe you'll drown." She wouldn't look at me on the elevator, staring at her phone instead, typing something frantically.

"What did your phone ever do to deserve that kind of punishment?" I asked, staring straight ahead.

"It's either type like this or wrap my hands around your throat."

"Be careful, Poison. For all you know, I might enjoy it." Why? Why did stupid shit like that come out of my mouth when I was around her?

She barely stopped short of shoving me aside to exit the elevator before I could, then almost ran down a pair of teenagers on their way down the hall.

"I still need the key," I called out behind her. Was I enjoying her little fit? More than I should. This was the first pleasure she'd given me since the night of Colton's wedding. I deserved it after the indignity of being babysat for two weeks.

The pleasure of watching her hips sway wasn't bad, either.

Fuck. We'd be sharing a room, and the woman wanted to kill me. I doubted that was hyperbole. There was no room for thoughts about her ass unless I was in the mood for a miserable hard-on all night.

A gasp rang out as soon as she pushed the door open while I was still a few rooms down the hall. "You're kidding me," she groaned out.

Once I rounded the doorframe, I understood. The chances of a painful hard-on were improving by the minute. "There's only one bed in the room," I observed in disbelief.

If my dick didn't thicken at the idea of sharing a bed with her, I might have laughed at the absurdity.

She didn't see the humor. "Congratulations." Ivy dropped onto the foot of the bed, arms folded. "You can count to one."

8

IVY

This was it. The straw that officially broke the camel's back. Sitting in a beautiful room in a beautiful lodge, forced to stay with a man whose skills in bed in no way outweighed his capacity for being a vindictive asswipe.

"I hope you're proud of yourself." I couldn't look at him. My entire body was so tight and tense I could barely move. It took everything I had not to start screaming and maybe break a few things for good measure.

"It doesn't have to be so bad," he offered with a shrug after closing the door. The man lived on another planet. That was the only explanation I could come up with for his blasé attitude. "Everybody was pleasant and helpful about sharing rooms."

"Stop talking," I warned. He had the nerve to wander the room and make it sound like I was being irrational. My heart was breaking, and I was on the verge of collapse after working my ass off to put this together in no time, but this spoiled baby couldn't let me succeed without throwing one more wrench into the works just because he could.

"You can always stay with one of your friends." He set his bag on the bed and unzipped it as he spoke, already getting himself settled in. "That Brad guy would share his room with you," he mused with a nasty little chuckle like it was all a big joke.

"I'm pretty sure I told you to stop talking." My head snapped up so I could glare at him even as I fought back frustrated, weary tears. "And you have no right to make jokes like that. Why don't you go and stay with Brad, instead? Or literally anyone else but me."

I might as well have recommended major surgery with no anesthesia. "News flash… it's not going to happen."

"Right. Because you are so much better than everybody here." The worst part was he didn't bother contradicting me, only lifting a shoulder as he began to unpack.

"Stop." I groaned. "We are not sharing this room, and we are not sharing a bed."

"We've done it before," he reminded me with a knowing laugh that made me wonder how he'd look with only one eye after I clawed the other one out.

And yet, my entire body insisted on reacting favorably to the memory. It didn't matter what my brain thought about it. A shiver ran through me and made goose bumps race up and down my arms while heat exploded in my core. *Not the time, not the time. He's literally the devil.*

"That was then," I reminded him back. "Like I told you, I didn't know at the time we would be working together, and neither did you."

"You're still going with that argument, Poison?"

I would lose teeth before much longer if I kept grinding them every time he called me that. "So help me, God, I will throw you out," I whispered. When he had the nerve to snort, I stood and held him in place with my unblinking stare. "Try me."

"Okay, for fuck's sake." He raised his hands like I was holding him up. "Things have happened, but you know, we might actually be able to enjoy ourselves."

"Unlikely." A horrible thought crossed my mind and almost made me forget how furious I was. "We can't have people knowing we share a room. This isn't going to work. You have to go."

"Nobody needs to know. Unless you decide to start bitching about it to your friends."

"I have more important things to worry about. Such as keeping this whole event on track." When he didn't seem impressed, I added, "You know, you don't even have to be here. Why are you here, anyway?"

He paused in the middle of placing socks in the dresser. "This is my company."

"It's your father's company," I reminded him. He could pretend, but I wasn't fooled. The reminder irked him to no end. "And considering how you think you're so far above sharing a room with one of your employees, I can't imagine you getting anything out of the experience."

"Let me worry about what I'm going to get out of the experience." He slammed the suitcase shut, his jaw tightening. "You worry about everything else. And don't worry about what will happen if we have to share this king-size bed. Right now, I wouldn't touch you on a dare, Poison." He had a talent for sounding brutally dismissive.

"So long as nobody knows," I reminded him, and his only response was a sigh.

What could I do? Short of killing him, which was still not completely off the table, I had no choice but to accept this infuriating turn of events. Since we were already running late, and my schedule for the evening was completely screwed as a result, there was no time to hash things out. "I need to get down to the banquet room. I need to make sure everything's all set for dinner."

"Don't let me stop you."

I knew I should walk away, at least let myself cool down a little before I said anything that would get me fired. Then again, I had already said more than enough that would've had me packing my things under any other circumstances. Somehow, I was still employed.

"I just want to know why." With my hand on the doorknob, I turned to him. He had the nerve to arch an eyebrow like he was genuinely unconcerned. "Why did you do that? Why go out of your way to sabotage me? I wouldn't have done it to you."

His features shifted, and for a second there, I thought he might genuinely feel sorry, but it didn't last long. By the time he took a breath to speak, he was wearing the same unconcerned expression. "Maybe you deserved it after undermining me."

"After you cut me out of that meeting," I reminded him, my voice shaking with barely suppressed hatred. That was the excuse he was going with? "You know, it's no wonder your father didn't trust you to run things on your own because you are a complete child."

Satisfaction spread through me at the sight of his jaw falling open as I made my exit. Good. Let him figure out he's not playing games with somebody who would turn the other cheek when he insisted on acting like a bastard.

I only wished I didn't feel slightly bad about saying it as I hurried down the hall on my way to the banquet room. If his feelings were hurt, he deserved it. Maybe he would learn not to cross me. Though, I doubted anybody had ever stood up to him the way I did.

Either way, he was old enough to handle it.

∽

"Thank you all so much for bearing with us tonight." When the room erupted in applause, I took a tiny bow. It was almost surreal. Standing in front of so many people, trying to keep the energy high and positive, I felt Lucian's eyes on me throughout my little speech after dinner.

Let him stare at me now while sixty of his supposed employees applauded me.

"You're all free to explore the lodge," I announced. "There's a nice lounge down the hall, in case you haven't visited yet, and a game room past the lobby. The weather is supposed to be much better tomorrow, so it looks like we'll be able to get out there for a hike before our mixer tomorrow night."

There were a few whistles of appreciation when I brought that up. Somehow, Cynthia had managed to call in a favor and arranged for a popular band to perform at the party scheduled for Saturday night. There would be dancing, drinking, and unwinding after a day spent together.

Everybody seemed to be in good spirits by the time we broke up for the night, with some people talking about heading to the lounge while others seemed more interested in heading back to their rooms. I would've liked to go back to my room. I was exhausted and knew exactly the kind of long day I had ahead of me. What a shame I would have rather chopped off my hand than spend another minute with a vile piece of shit who wasted no time heading out after the post-dinner meeting was over.

"Why even bother coming?" I heard the question and turned to find the speaker, who was none other than Molly Kramer from Jones. "It's obvious he has better things to do."

Oh, how much did I want to agree with her? She didn't have a clue just how far the man could sink. I could tell her stories that would curl her hair—one of Mom's old sayings.

Thinking of her reminded me I had promised to call once things had wrapped up for the night. It also reminded me I still needed to play nice, even if Lucian was making it harder every damn day.

"I'm sure he's got other things on his mind," I pointed out as I approached the cluster of women hanging out near the doorway. "Not everybody in his position would join in on something like this. Let's give him the benefit of the doubt."

The words practically curdled in my mouth, but everybody seemed to accept them, even blushing and looking at the floor like they were embarrassed after getting caught. "So, what do you think of your rooms?" I asked, changing the subject when it was obvious I had made everybody uncomfortable. I was still getting the hang of this whole managerial thing, though I knew damn well I was better at it than Lucian could ever hope to be.

Funny, but I was dreading being alone with him only minutes ago. Now, I could hardly wait to point out what an uncooperative prick he was.

After saying good night to everybody still hanging around, I trekked through the lobby to the elevator. The lodge was more like a small city. I had scheduled free time tomorrow at Cynthia's suggestion and now considered visiting the spa on the premises. If there were anybody in history who deserved a massage, it was me. The idea danced around in my head as I waited for one of the two elevators to arrive.

"There you are." I recognized Brad's voice before turning to find him coming my way. The rustic surroundings made him look even more like a model about to do something outdoorsy for a photo shoot. "Going back up so soon? I thought for sure you'd want to hang out, grab a drink with us."

Was there any nice way to tell him I wanted almost nothing less than I wanted to do what he described? Sure, the alternative was going upstairs and facing Lucian, but at least then I wouldn't have to pretend to be in a better mood than I was. I didn't have it in me to be social, and it was that prick's fault.

"I'm wiped," I confessed with a weak shrug. "And I have so much to go over before tomorrow. I wouldn't be any fun, anyway."

"You don't know that." His blue eyes searched my face like he was looking for a hint of encouragement.

"I don't know how I feel?" I tipped my head to the side and watched his face fall. "I think I know how I feel, Brad."

"I didn't mean it that way. I'm sorry, I'm messing this up." He ran a hand through his blond hair and sighed. "I was hoping you wanted to hang out. That's all."

"I'm awfully sorry to disappoint you." I had to tread carefully. This would be a lot easier if I didn't know he liked me. The saddest part was how I craved someone simple and uncomplicated like Brad. I knew where I stood. There was no screwing around, no games.

But I was his superior, which meant a whole other set of problems. That, and he had never sparked anything in me. We had no chemistry, unlike Lucian and me. "I'll see you first thing in the morning at breakfast. And have fun," I encouraged once the elevator doors finally opened so I could make my escape. "That's what this weekend is all about, right?"

He didn't look convinced. If anything, he looked even more disappointed than he was before. What? Did he think this would be the weekend when we finally got together? Oh, no, I hoped not.

One thing at a time.

My immediate problem was figuring out a way to coexist with Lucian without committing homicide. Not that I particularly cared whether he lived or died at the moment, but Mom needed me. I wouldn't be much good to her in a prison cell.

My feet were lead blocks, but I dragged myself down the hallway anyway, my heart pounding in anticipation of what was to come. If only it didn't feel like I was preparing for battle.

The shower was running when I opened the door to the room. He was humming in there, the prick. He even managed to sound happy. A man without a care in the world. That was how he had always lived, wasn't it? And he had the audacity to sabotage me when he had lived life on easy mode all along.

While he was safely behind a closed door, I quickly unpacked since I didn't have a lot of time to do it earlier. I was also feeling more than a little stubborn. Unpacking meant admitting there was no getting out of this situation. Fighting against it was a waste of time, though, and I didn't want to make an ass out of myself by refusing to make myself comfortable on principle.

How were we supposed to share a bed, and why the hell

did my body insist on tingling at the thought? Okay, so there was no real question there. The night we spent together was probably the hottest ever. It would be stupid of me, unforgivably stupid if I gave in to my body's urges.

Lucian Diamond wasn't just dangerous as far as my career was concerned. He was a walking nuclear bomb that could blow everything up and leave me scrambling to pick up the burned pieces. No amount of sex was worth that, no matter how good. *Stop thinking about it, you idiot.*

The shower turned off, giving me no choice but to step out onto the balcony to call Mom without him hanging over my shoulder. The night air was fresh and clear after all that rain. The clouds were breaking up, giving me a glimpse of a starry sky and a three-quarter moon.

It was gorgeous up here. I had no idea it was possible for this many stars to be visible. Too much time spent in the city.

Unfortunately, Mom didn't answer. I was worried when I called the nurses' station, but they assured me she was fine and had gone to sleep a little earlier than usual. At least I knew she was all right, even if I hated the idea of being all the way up here when literally anything might happen. "Please, don't decide to get out of bed on your own again," I whispered to my phone before tucking it into my pocket and taking a few deep breaths of the sweet night air. We had gotten off lucky earlier in the week. She hadn't broken anything. Her luck had to run out sometime.

Unless I went to sleep out here on the balcony, I couldn't avoid Lucian forever. Funny how the idea actually appealed to me for a second or two as I squared my shoulders and stiffened my spine.

Time for the next round in this endless battle.

9

LUCIAN

"I thought you were going to stay out there all night, Poison." From my position on the bed, where I had settled in and was now flipping through television channels, I had the pleasure of seeing her scowl.

"Making yourself comfortable already?" Her scowl deepened.

"Sure. What, was I supposed to go down there and rub elbows with everybody else?"

"You know, it wouldn't break your neck to do that."

"It wouldn't break my neck to do a lot of things, but that doesn't mean I have to do them. I know you're supposed to be my babysitter around the office, but do you have to sound like my mother too, Poison?"

Her nostrils flared the way they sometimes did when I called her that. "When you insist on acting like a child? I can't help it."

"Come on. Why don't we try to start over?"

She chuckled, standing with her back to the television and blocking my view. Not that it mattered. She was much more interesting. "Fine. I would be glad to. But only if you tell me the truth about how those rooms ended up being released."

"You heard the girl at the desk. Somebody called and said we didn't need them." She rolled her eyes. "Didn't we have this discussion earlier, anyway? You made a little quip about me and my father, if I remember correctly."

"I need to hear you say it."

It wasn't like she could do anything to me. "Fine. Yes, I made the call."

"You fucking bastard!"

"I gave you what you wanted, right?" When a tissue box sailed through the air and hit the wall above my head, I sat up straight. "Listen up. Fun is fun, but that doesn't mean you throw things at me."

"Fun?" She burst out laughing—high-pitched, humorless. "You are a piece of work. Tell me, what's so fun about having to scramble around and find an alternative after you fucked me over? Was that fun for you? Because it sure as hell wasn't for me."

"Well, should've thought about that—"

"Enough," she grunted out through clenched teeth, cutting off anything else I was about to say. "You're not going to gaslight me into thinking anything about this is okay."

"Now I'm a gaslighter?" I murmured, looking around like I was confused. "I've never heard that one before."

Either she was too furious to hear me or didn't care to acknowledge it. "I am sorry if you don't like working around me. I am. It kind of sucks when there's no choice but to go along with the shit you don't want to do, doesn't it? Guess what?" She threw her arms into the air. "That's how the rest of the world lives. I don't deserve to be treated like a joke because you can't handle being treated like a regular, normal person. And let's not even pretend you live like the rest of us!" she continued while I could only stare at her in disbelief. "You are still nowhere near the sort of life we live. Do you think it's in any way normal for somebody with no experience to be promoted to vice president of an entire division in a huge company? Do you think that's really the way the world works for anybody but you?"

She was lucky her sanctimonious bullshit didn't get her thrown out of the lodge after I fired her smart ass. "Spare me the working man sob story and admit you're pissy because I fucked with your retreat. I knew you would find a way out of it. And you did, so no harm was done."

She folded her arms and popped one hip out to the side. Her lips pursed as she looked me up and down. Damn. Even now, staring daggers, she was blisteringly hot. "Sure. No harm was done. If it makes you feel better, tell yourself that."

She went to the closet and flung the door open. From where I stretched out on the bed, I could see her reach inside and pull out an arm full of extra pillows.

"What's that for?" I asked.

"What do you think?" She yanked the blankets back on the other side of the bed, muttering to herself as she placed the pillows in a line down the center to separate us.

"You can't be serious," I laughed, but she kept working. "You're splitting the bed in half?"

"Yes, I am." When she was finished, she pulled clothes from one of the dresser drawers and marched to the bathroom. "I'm going straight to bed when I come out. Don't talk to me."

I would have laughed that off if it hadn't been for the tremor in her voice when she said it. Brief, barely noticeable, but present. The sound of somebody who might've been on the verge of tears.

I could deal with a lot of things, but a crying woman? I wasn't strong enough to handle that. Now that we were alone and the first night of the retreat was over, and it sounded like she might be crying in the bathroom, I realized I couldn't remember why it was so important to screw with her plans. She had pissed me off, yes, but childish shit like that was beneath me. Wasn't it? I had always thought so. I wasn't so sure anymore, and I didn't know what to think about that.

I was glad for a phone call to distract me, at least until I saw who was calling. It shouldn't have come as any surprise. Dad didn't want to be here, but he wanted to keep tabs. Par for the course. "Everything's fine," I told him after the usual small talk. "We were held up by the weather, but it all worked out."

"Glad to hear that. Do me a favor, would you?" he asked. I could hear the ice clinking in his glass. He could afford to sit back and relax with a drink, miles away from this farce.

I closed my eyes, bracing myself. Nothing good ever followed that question. "I'll do what I can."

"Get along with Ivy. Cynthia told me the girl is in knots over this. She wants so much to make life easier for the newcomers. She said that's all Ivy could talk about this week as they worked together. Making sure everybody felt comfortable, since there was such a culture shock going from a little nothing operation like Jones to what we've built. It's overwhelming for them."

"Cynthia told you that?"

"She did. And from what I understand, Ivy is nervous about her mother. Being so far away from her all weekend when she lives in a nursing facility. I know you don't like Ivy—"

"I never said I didn't like her." Fuck, was there anything

worse than hearing him talk to me like the child Ivy thought I was? Yes, as a matter of fact.

Ivy's mom was alone in a nursing home, and instead of spending time with her this weekend, she decided to bring our employees together. And I had tried to sabotage that.

"Just the same. Take it easy on her. Maybe try to help her out a little. That's what leaders do."

I couldn't have felt smaller if I tried. Like an insect. "I'll do what I can."

The shower turned off, and I knew better than to stay on the phone until she emerged. What would Dad do if she came out screaming mad and he heard her? "I better go. We have a long day tomorrow, and I want to rest up."

"A wise decision." Dammit, how did he manage to sound so condescending? My knee-jerk reaction was to consider heading down to the lounge just to defy him. How twisted was that?

I was still stewing over the impulse to defy him. However, I knew I'd only end up hurting myself by adding a hangover to the list of reasons I wasn't looking forward to tomorrow when the bathroom door opened and Ivy emerged. She had changed into a worn-out tee and loose cotton shorts that revealed a lot more of her legs than I was used to seeing around the office.

Don't stare, do not fucking stare. I gripped the duvet in my fists, staring at the television without seeing a damn thing on the screen as she settled into bed, making a big deal of punching her pillow like it had offended her before she slammed her head onto it with her back turned to me.

Don't look, do not look. I didn't need to. She was right there, a few feet away, smelling like coconut and lime, thanks to whatever she used in the shower. Her hair was back in a bun, and my fingers twitched, longing to reach out and stroke a few strands that had fallen loose just to remember its softness.

"I guess I should go." Her body gleamed like a pearl in the moonlight. She sat up, stretching once the sheet fell away. Hunger flared up the second I looked at her, watching her body move. The full, perfect tits that swayed a little when she stretched again. The graceful line of her throat and slim shoulders. She was perfect, a masterpiece carved from marble, but very warm and very real.

And very, very wanted. "Who said?" I propped myself up on one elbow, grinning when her eyes met mine from across the bed. She didn't believe me.

"I didn't think you would ask me to spend the entire night."

"Nobody said anything about the entire night," I teased. It was fun making her blush. When we met at the country club, she gave off the impression of a girl with her shit together. Smart, unwilling to accept any bullshit lines from guys looking to get in her panties. She had made me work for it a little, teasing and challenging me as we flirted. What a fucking turn-on that was.

"Oh?" She turned to me, leaning in until her nipples brushed my chest and her mouth hovered inches from mine. I almost forgot to breathe, too overwhelmed at her nearness to do more than go hard in an instant. "You think you can handle another round? I figured I would've exhausted you by now."

Rather than say a word, I took her hand and placed it over my very obvious erection. "Think again."

And then I was on her, flipping her onto her back and settling over her squirming, soft body. "You think it's that easy?" She giggled, squealing when I tried to part her legs.

"You tell me." With one hand, I caressed her, letting my fingers trail over her throat, skimming her collarbone before moving lower. She melted like butter on a hot pan, arching her back, releasing a sigh that turned to a gasp when I brushed over

her taut nipple. "Seems like it's pretty easy to warm you up," I whispered, lowering my head to take her rosy peak between my lips.

"Oh, my God..." The pressure of her hand on the back of my head was exhilarating, and the feeling only got more intense when her fingers began dancing through my hair. "How are you so good at that?"

I was good at this because we were good together. There was more going on here than me finding a way to get off as efficiently as possible after making a woman come, and I always made it a point to take care of that first.

I didn't want to only make her come. I wanted to see how far I could take her. How many times she could shatter around me. How many times I could reduce her to a panting, sweaty mess. There was a rush involved, something bigger than anything I had ever known. I wanted to have her in every way possible, as many times as possible.

She let out a disappointed little groan when I released her nipple with a soft popping sound, but that sound turned to a satisfied sigh when I rolled her onto her stomach. I had never seen an ass like hers. My fingers pressed against her flesh, the excitement building in me while she moaned her approval.

"Touch me," she begged in a harsh whisper, turning her head and meeting my gaze with eyes that blazed with need. She spread her thighs and lifted her ass, revealing her smooth, plump lips and the juices already glistening on them. I dragged a finger through that wetness, and she moaned again, rolling her hips and making my cock drip with excitement.

I reached over into the nightstand drawer where the pack of condoms waited, pulling another from the box and quickly unrolling it down my length. "You think this sweet pussy can take another pounding?" I asked as I dragged my head through her drenched folds.

"Yes," she whispered, gripping the pillow under her head like she was bracing herself for what she knew was coming. "Yes, please."

"Please, what, Ivy?" I was her king, her god, controlling every moment of her pleasure, teasing her clit with my dick, running it across her quivering hole. Promising so much but delivering nothing until I was damn ready.

"Please, fuck me," she pleaded so sweetly that I had no choice but to give her what she wanted. And hard.

Sure. That was exactly what I needed to be thinking of. Now I had a painfully erect dick to contend with, along with the presence of a woman who would rather pitch herself off that balcony than endure my touch. I did it to myself, that much I could admit, if only to me.

At least she couldn't see the tent I was making, still facing away from me as I turned out the light on my side of the bed and settled in, turning my back on her. "I usually sleep with the TV on," I muttered, turning down the volume for her sake.

"That's fine," she muttered back. "I do too. Most of the time."

It didn't seem right, ending the night like that. I was starting to feel like a real piece of shit over the stunt I pulled. I couldn't call it a prank in good conscience. I had wanted to fuck up her plans and had done it out of spite like some bratty kid.

"You did a good job today," I offered, closing my eyes and willing myself to ignore the absolute bitch of an erection threatening to consume my every thought. I was a grown man and could handle it, so long as I stopped reminiscing about the tightness of her pussy, the way she creamed all over me.

She kept me waiting long enough that I wondered if she had fallen asleep. Eventually, she grunted, "Thanks."

I could count on one hand the number of times I'd done something I truly regretted, and this situation marked one of them. We could be wrapped up in each other this very minute if I hadn't gone out of my way to drive a wedge between us. Who cared about a working relationship? What we had shared went beyond that. There was no forgetting our instant connection and how well we fit together.

Not that it mattered now that I had taken our rivalry too far. All I had to show for myself was a painful hard-on and more than a few regrets which had to do with more than my cock. My conscience was beating the shit out of me too. I had acted based on assumptions, and it looked more and more like my assumptions were wrong. She wasn't trying to steal anything from me unless being talented and gifted when it came to managing people were her weapons.

I had fucked everything up and hurt her in the process.

Now, to find a way to make it up to her… if it wasn't too late.

10

IVY

The difference in Lucian between Friday and Saturday was astounding. Something had lit a fire under him, only I didn't know what.

At first, I didn't know whether to take him seriously. By the time I woke up on Saturday morning, there was a cup of coffee from the café in the lobby waiting for me on the nightstand. It was the aroma that woke me up before my alarm ever sounded. Either I had slept like the dead, or he was the quietest person who ever lived.

People were already gathering in the banquet room for breakfast by the time I made it down, and Lucian was hanging around the buffet table, chatting with everybody as they took their food. He was like a different person, chuckling over the incredible water pressure in the showers, offering ideas for what to do during our scheduled free time in the afternoon since he was so familiar with the lodge and the area. I said nothing, settling for a brief glance as I took my plate to an empty chair beside Laney.

"I was wondering where you were," she said as soon as I sat. "I figured you would be the first person down here."

"I must have passed out cold," I confess. "I guess I haven't gotten enough sleep lately. Between planning this and worrying about Mom..."

"Well, you slept a lot better than I did. Barbara has a snoring problem." Laney rolled her eyes, her gaze traveling over to where Barbara chatted at another table with a few of the older ladies. It was nice to see her blending in so well with the long-time Diamond employees.

"I'm sorry for the way the sleeping arrangements panned out." There must've been something about the air in the Catskills because I was ravenous, digging into scrambled eggs and French toast with abandon. Was I going to tell her about my sleeping arrangements? Absolutely not.

"It is what it is." She sighed. "I intend to get drunk enough tonight at the party that it won't matter how loud she snores. I'll be out like a light."

Giggling, she held up crossed fingers. "I hope you manage to have a little fun. You deserve it after putting so much work into this."

"Good morning, ladies." Brad offered us both a warm grin as he sat across from me, dressed in a T-shirt, cargo pants, and hiking boots. Was he granting me space? He usually didn't bother with that, but it was a welcome relief all the same. I should have given him an attitude sooner. "Looking forward to our hike? It looks great out there today."

"I know I could use some time in the fresh air," I confess. "I'm sure my skin won't know what to do under the sun when it spends so much time under fluorescent bulbs."

"I hope you brought sunscreen." Out of nowhere appeared Lucian, wearing a smile that didn't reach his eyes. No, they were hard and calculating, and they kept landing on Brad. "Don't want to get burned."

"I'm always careful not to get burned," I assured him, making his mouth twitch like he caught my double meaning. Did I sound as nervous as I felt? My nerves were jangling, my stomach was suddenly too full, and my heart was pounding in my ears. Why did he come over here? Where was this leading?

He jerked his chin at Brad, and I damn near threw up. Don't say anything stupid, please. "I heard you were kicking ass last night at the pool table in the games room," he said.

Brad chuckled, shrugging. "I misspent a lot of hours at the pool hall when I was a kid."

"We'll have to shoot a game before the weekend's over. I wasted a lot of time around a pool table, myself." With that, he smiled at all of us then moved on to the next table.

"Wonders never cease. Somebody decided to participate," Laney mused, watching him closely as he moved through the room. "God, he is gorgeous."

"Girl talk? I think I'll pass." Brad rolled his eyes, snickering at us as he got up and mercifully walked away. His presence didn't always irk me the way it did now. What changed? And why did it set my teeth on edge to watch Laney follow Lucian around the room with her eyes?

∾

"I THOUGHT you said this was going to be a hike. It's more like a walk." Laney looked behind us at the clusters of coworkers making their way down the path. "Not that I'm complaining. I hate hiking."

"All right, so I might have exaggerated a little when I called it a hike," I confessed in a whisper. "I couldn't call it a group walk, you know. It just didn't sound right. Besides, I'm sure the older people won't mind."

The nice, leisurely stroll through a shaded, beautifully landscaped path was pleasant, even refreshing. The humidity that had been such a problem in the city was practically nonexistent up here, and the air was crystal clear. Everybody seemed to be in a good mood too. This was working.

"Ow!"

I should've known.

The shout was so sudden it made me jump before I spun around and found Molly Kegan on the ground a few dozen feet behind me. A handful of people clustered around her while she grabbed her ankle and winced. "I stumbled over a rock and twisted it," she explained, wincing again at her scraped palms.

Lucian's voice rang out behind me, coming closer. "Let me in here." I watched, stunned into silence, as he nudged his way through the crowd.

"I'm such an idiot," Molly grumbled while he gently moved her hands away from her ankle so he could take a look. It already looked thicker than it should, and she sucked in a breath when he touched it.

"All right," he announced. "We need to get this shoe off before your foot swells too much. It's going to hurt a lot worse if we wait."

"I'm completely in your hands," she told him. Was I imagining the way her voice sounded different now? Softer. It wasn't easy to pry my gaze away from him. Fuck, it was hot watching him jump into action to observe her. She would've gladly broken a bone to earn even more attention, practically batting her eyelashes and swooning.

And she wasn't the only one. I glanced around, sizing up the reactions of the other women. They all either looked like they wanted to melt or, in Barbara's case, pinch his cheeks, maybe after melting.

"Let's get you back to the lodge. One second." Lucian pulled out his phone and chose a contact before holding the device to his ear. "This is Lucian Diamond. I'm bringing an injured woman back to the lodge after walking on the trail. It's not an emergency," he explained, giving Molly a little wink. "I would like an Ace bandage and an ice pack on arrival. I'm going to bring her back up right now."

"You really don't have to do that," Molly protested, but it was weak at best. Her eyes were practically twinkling at this point while Chuck and Brad helped her stand on her good leg.

"Sure, I do." Then, as if the entire experience wasn't already enough to make me want to drop my panties, he picked her up. "Let's go. Sorry to leave you all," Lucian called out over his shoulder.

"Holy shit." Laney leaned against me and heaved a quiet sigh. "That might have been the hottest thing I've ever seen."

Same here.

∽

"No, really. I'm beat!" I was about to turn into the girl who took her shoes off in public because they were aching after I'd danced my ass off for three hours. The band was great, the drinks were potent, and I deserved it.

"Stay down here with us!" Laney draped an arm around my waist and tried to steer me toward the lounge, which would be open for another hour or so. A bunch of people were headed that way now that the party was over, and my heart just about burst when I noticed the way everybody mingled like old friends. Put enough booze in people, get some good music playing, and magic happened.

I wanted to stay with them if only to keep soaking in this good feeling, but I was already walking the line between tipsy and drunk and didn't want to go any further. "Honestly, I am wiped out. What I need more than anything is a shower and bed."

"Boo!" She cupped her hands around her mouth and shouted it again. I could only laugh and shake my head, turning toward the lobby. Everybody would keep having a great time without me, and that was okay. After a day full of hanging out together outdoors, visiting the spa, shooting pool, and playing air hockey and old-school arcade games, I was more than ready for sleep.

The most pleasant surprise of this weekend was, of course, Lucian. I wasn't surprised that he didn't dance along with the rest of us, but he did hang out, have a few drinks, and generally seemed to enjoy himself. He shot pool with Brad earlier, played air hockey with Chuck and a couple of the other guys, and had granted me a wide berth the entire day. I hadn't even run into him in our room before dinner and the party following.

The less time we spent together, the better since there was less chance of him saying anything unforgivably stupid or me rising to the bait and barely stopping short of biting his head off.

Right now, though, I didn't want to avoid him. I wanted to thank him for playing along all day and jumping into action when Molly got hurt. In fact, I was feeling so much warmer toward him by the time I took the elevator up to the fourth floor. I was glad I hadn't gone to the lounge for another drink or two. I was already dangerously close to liking him. Add too much vodka into the mix, and things could get dicey. And naked.

Remember how he's treated you. Yes, that was a good idea. He thought I slept with him to get ahead at work. Accused me of kissing ass around the office. He had rescheduled my meeting and sabotaged the retreat. And that was only the stuff I knew about.

I was feeling considerably less pleasant as I opened the door to the room, but that was for the best. Another night spent with pillows between us wouldn't kill me. By this time tomorrow, we would be home, and it would all be behind us.

"There you are." He was on his way in from the balcony, phone in hand. The night breeze had tousled his dark hair, and he raked it back from his forehead. "I was going to send a search party for you if you didn't come up soon. I thought maybe Brad cornered you."

This again. "I'm starting to think you're jealous." I dropped my shoes on the floor and plopped onto the bed, flexing my feet and groaning.

"Please…" he snickered, "… he's a douche."

"A douche you were hanging around with earlier, or was that some other rich kid shooting pool over beers this afternoon?" I couldn't help but laugh when he rolled his eyes.

"I'm not a kid," he growled out.

"That's the part you take offense to?"

"Why would I be offended by being called rich? I am." Leaning against the dresser, he folded his arms and eyed my bare feet. "You're not a bad dancer. You should dance more often."

I couldn't keep up with the way his train of thought kept bouncing back and forth. "Thanks. I guess you aren't a good dancer?"

"Why do you say that?"

"Because you didn't dance, genius."

Snickering, he said, "Not my thing. I would rather get a workout some other way, Poison."

Damn. He didn't even have to come out and be blatant about it. All it took was the slightest suggestive comment, and my body decided to stage a revolt. I would have to ignore my quickening pulse and the goose bumps that rose over my legs and arms. So what if my breath caught and my pussy went hot?

"Would you look at that." He checked his obscenely beautiful watch, which, from the looks of it, cost a fortune, and his eyebrows shot up. "It's been an entire three minutes, and we're still getting along."

"It must be all the endorphins from the dancing," I suggested while my clit began to ache. He was here, only a few feet away, and I knew from experience how incredible he was. He obviously wanted this. I couldn't betray myself and give in, could I?

His smirk turned to a full-blown and painfully sexy smile. "You want endorphins? I can give you some endorphins."

"You have a one-track mind tonight, don't you?"

Lowering his brow, he growled out, "I have a one-track mind every night."

A shiver raced through me, and I'd swear my heart was going to burst out of my chest. Were we really doing this? "I don't find that hard to believe." *Don't do this. You work together. He's kind of your boss.* "If I didn't know better, I would think you were so nice today just to get on my good side. Like you wanted to wear me down before you got me here tonight."

Unfolding his arms, he stood up straight, placed his hands on his hips, and loomed over me. "I'm honestly disappointed."

My stomach did a slow flip, and my toes practically curled. Dear God, was I actually considering lying back and letting him do whatever he wanted all because he now had that whole stern disciplinarian energy going on? I didn't think those drinks were that strong. "It was only a joke," I choked out. "Sorry."

"Maybe I was trying to make it up to you after yesterday. Maybe I felt sorry for fucking around when you put so much work into this and care so much. You did a great job with this event, and it was a good idea." One corner of his mouth quirked upward as he asked, "Though if I were deliberately doing this to get in your panties, would it work?"

"You are ridiculous." And so was I, for that matter. Suddenly, I was way too aware of my dress riding up my thighs, my hardening nipples, and how damn thick his thighs were. And his hands, oh fuck. My skin craved the feel of them.

His dark eyes flashed. "And you are looking at me like you want me to take your clothes off with my teeth."

My mouth went dry, not that I could talk anyway since my throat closed up until I could barely take a sip of air. My chest heaved from the effort of trying to breathe as he slowly lowered himself to his knees in front of me.

"Well, Poison?" he murmured, taking my left ankle in one hand, then pressing his thumb against my sore arch. I gasped, my body going stiff before melting because, damn, that was good.

"Well, what?" I whispered, shaky. I was on the edge of a cliff, and he was standing behind me, ready to push me over the edge.

"Do you or do you not want me to take your clothes off with my teeth? I mean, I can use my hands if you would rather." His other hand encircled my ankle before he began sliding it up my calf. "Don't act like you weren't eye fucking me all night. Watching me. Every time I found you in the crowd, you were already staring at me."

"Your ego—" I sucked in another gasp when he stroked the inside of my knee.

I was gone.

I never had a chance of winning.

This was the ultimate game, and he didn't believe in following the rules.

"My ego is big, but it's not nearly as big as my dick, Poison. You know all about that." Still stroking that ultrasensitive patch of skin, he leaned in, his breath hitting my face and smelling like whiskey. That, plus his insanely sexy, leathery cologne, was hot enough to melt any last lingering resistance. "Now don't tell me you can look at this big bed and not imagine putting it to good use. And I'm not talking about sleep."

"You're not playing fair."

"Who said I was trying to?" His dark, dangerous eyes landed on my mouth. Silently questioning, telling me what he wanted to do next.

Were we doing this? Did we ever have a choice?

All it took was me biting ever so slightly on my bottom lip to make him lunge forward, his mouth meeting mine a second before his hand cupped the back of my neck.

Fireworks. They exploded in my head, every color of the rainbow, filling my body with searing heat. If this was all wrong, why did it feel so good?

It was better than before. The same intense lust flared up between us, but there was urgency now. Like we were both back where we wanted to be after too long holding back and couldn't wait. It was enough to make me forget the resentment, the bitterness, everything but this.

His soft grunts and the slow stroking of his tongue against mine were incredible but not nearly as good as the feel of his hands on my legs, sliding the dress up to my hips, pushing my knees apart. Yes, this, more of this. Now that it was happening, I wanted everything, all of him.

I dropped back onto the bed, my hands sliding over the silk duvet as I lifted my head while he slowly and reverently slid my panties down my thighs, then over my knees. The scrap of black lace hit the floor before he draped my legs over his shoulders.

We exchanged one brief glance then he began kissing his way up the sides of my thighs, using his tongue to trace slow, sensual circles over my skin. By the time he reached my shaved mound, I was practically lifting my hips, offering myself to him.

He growled, the scruff of his cheeks chafing my thighs. "I've missed this pretty pussy." His tongue slid up the length of my swollen slit, and I almost howled. I was already so close, like a coiled spring ready to pop. All it took was a few laps of that skillful tongue to push me over the edge.

Even I couldn't believe it, laughing between helpless moans. Lucian seemed to take it as a challenge, working to keep me hovering in that blissed-out place, practically devouring me like an animal as he claimed every inch of my pussy for himself.

And I wanted him to. Taking the back of his head in my hand, I pulled him closer, demanding more. His deep, throaty chuckle sent delicious vibrations racing through me while the tension in my core built again. He worked his fingers inside me, stretching me while flicking my clit with the tip of his tongue.

"Yes, just like that," I pleaded in a whisper, panting for air, my body straining. "Don't stop. So close. *Don't stop...*" A violent sob tore its way from me when the wave broke, submerging me in peaceful darkness for a few moments. It rocked my body and soul, shockwaves rolling through me, the sensations going on and on. How did he do this to me? How was it so good?

I barely noticed him standing or heard his belt and zipper. My eyes opened in time to see his pants drop to the floor, then his boxer briefs along with them. The sight of his rigid, swaying cock was almost enough to scare me until I remembered taking him before. More than once.

There was a foil packet in his hand, and I sat up quickly and lowered the zipper on the side of my dress while he unrolled the latex down his shaft. He groaned once the dress was off, and I unclasped my bra, letting it fall away from my breasts. "Fuck, Poison. I only thought I remembered how perfect you are," he told me, eyes glued to my body.

A body that hummed under his gaze as I worked my way farther back on the bed. He followed, crawling up the length of my body. I caught his mouth with mine and kissed him while unbuttoning his shirt. Once it was open, I slid it over his shoulders and down his arms, then feasted on the feel of his chiseled muscles. How did I think I could work with him and never touch him again? It all seemed so pointless now, trying to keep away from him.

"You ready for this?" My eyes flew open wide when the head of his cock dragged through my slit, teasing my clit a little before moving back down to my entrance. "Tell me you want this."

"I want this," I whispered, moving my hips, trying to pull him inside me.

"How much?" he asked, teeth gritted like he was barely holding on.

I locked my legs around his hips and drew him closer. "With all of me. I need you with all of me. Please, Lucian..." I begged, straining upward.

He didn't hesitate, plunging deep inside me without warning, filling me the way only he could. My nails sank into his shoulders, but it was so good and even better when he pulled back to push forward again. There was no taking it slow and easy, not that I wanted to. I wanted him to take me back to the wild place we had found together, where he unlocked part of me I didn't know existed until that night. Something dark and primal.

"You're so good..." he grunted close to my ear, breathing faster with every stroke. "So tight. I'm going to need you to be a good girl for me."

One of his hands traveled down my side, fingers digging into my hip before he drove himself deep again. I whimpered in his ear, lost in pleasure. "Yes!"

"You're going to cream on my cock, Poison." He rolled his hips, and I gasped, clutching him closer, moving my hips in time with his. Close, so close, but I didn't want it to end. I didn't want it to ever end.

But it would have to. I didn't have a choice. My body was following its own rules, working for release. "Come for me, *now*," he rasped, barely holding on himself, losing his rhythm and pounding me wildly, making me scream until I had to press my mouth to his shoulder as I shattered in his arms.

He shuddered on top of me before pulling out and rolling away. All I could do was lie there, limp, drained. And relieved.

God, I needed that.

My next conscious thought?

I'm going to need that again.

Staring up at the ceiling, still trying to catch my breath, I said, "Nobody can know about this. I can't lose my job, and I can't jeopardize my future. Promise me."

"Nobody has to know." He rolled onto his side, still breathless and a little sweaty when I turned my head. "Only us," he promised.

"And it cannot affect work."

"It won't." He ran the backs of his fingers down my arm, making me shiver. I was still worked up and ultra-sensitive. "Now, I don't know about you, but I could use a shower. And there's more than enough room for two." The twinkle in his eyes made my heart skip a beat.

Dammit. I was in so much trouble.

11

LUCIAN

Suddenly, coming into the office was a lot more interesting.

I looked forward to it in the days following the retreat, which even I could admit was a success. Not that I cared about in-jokes or reminiscing over a marathon game of air hockey. Let the oblivious worker bees distract themselves with that.

All that interested me was the blonde who sat outside my office, someone much more pleasant to look at than my father. I'd spent enough time watching her while pretending otherwise to observe more than her beauty. She always had time for anyone who happened to pass by with a question or a problem. I had no idea how she managed to maintain her level of productivity while playing mother hen to her roost.

"You're in a good mood this morning." Dad narrowed his eyes at me over his cup of coffee during our Wednesday meeting. "That retreat must've done wonders for you. You came back here a changed man."

He always had to take it a step too far. " I've gone from a

caterpillar to a butterfly. Prepare to be dazzled by my transformation."

He waved me off dismissively. "All I'm saying is, I like what I see. I'm impressed. And the feedback from the retreat has been nothing but positive."

It was a funny thing. Most people would've been glad to have their father praise them like that. I hadn't exactly given him much of a reason to until now. The do-nothing son who coasted by in college and saw enough of the corporate world during his summer internships to know he wanted nothing to do with it. The son who showed no interest in controlling the family empire and laughed when he heard the word *legacy* being thrown around.

The ultimate disappointment...

... until now.

I should have been happy and pleased with myself, but instead, I shifted uncomfortably in my seat.

"And I'm pleased to see you turning into a good leader," he rambled on. "I understand you performed first aid on that girl who was injured on the hiking trail."

"First aid?" I scoffed. "She twisted her ankle. I carried her back to the lodge."

"You're a hero around here," he concluded.

This was torture. If I looked like a good leader during the retreat, it was all thanks to Ivy. Making up for the shit I pulled, trying to make things right between us. For the first time in a long time, I'd met someone whose esteem I would like to earn.

"I don't need the praise," I told him, taking a bite of my bagel. "And I don't need to be anybody's hero. You know how stories get inflated if given enough time."

"Fine, have it your way." He pursed his lips the way he

always did when there was something on his mind. "Have you given any thought to finding a serious relationship?"

I could have used a little warning. That way, I wouldn't have come close to choking. He waited until I was able to swallow my food before continuing, "It's something that's been weighing heavily on your mother's mind lately."

A deep gulp of my coffee washed down what nearly killed me before I said, "I thought these meetings were to discuss work, not my personal life."

"This is the only time during the week I'm sure I'll be able to get a few words in with you. You know how busy I am." I grunted. "She knows we meet on Wednesday mornings and told me to bring it up. What, are you suggesting I don't do something your mom ordered?"

For the first time all morning, we shared a genuine laugh. Mom could go from zero to nuclear in no time flat, completely tranquil to burning with anger. Dad had always loved her feistiness. So did I.

"I don't know what to tell you," I admitted. "It's not something I've given much thought to."

"Which is why your mom wants to think about it for you."

"No, thank you." Dad chuckled, but I didn't, staring at him so he would know I was serious. "I don't need anyone thinking about that for me. I'm not going to be forced into a relationship with a woman just because I've passed a certain number of birthdays. These things have to happen on their own, don't they? Just like you and Mom?"

"We're only worried you're missing out by playing the field."

Of all times for a familiar ice blonde head to fill my imagination. Playing the field had led to that first night with Ivy, and I would never regret it. Flirting at the bar, getting turned on by her wickedly quick wit. The ultimate foreplay. Would I ever meet another woman who could keep up with me in and out of bed?

Why the fuck was I thinking about her now?

"I'm sure I'll be fine. Mom will have her grandkids someday." For once, I was glad for the distraction of business. Sliding a handful of printed reports his way, I explained, "The latest analytics from our online publications in the Midwest. Clicks to our sites are going through the roof, and ad revenue along with it. Ivy and I have been focusing on the social media accounts of those publications, driving traffic that way. No clickbait," I added before he could ask. "Well-crafted posts that have people wanting to learn more."

His eyes widened when he compared this month's numbers to last month's. "The girl's got a good head on her shoulders. I'm glad you two are learning to work together. She's been a good influence on you."

He had no idea what a good influence she was. I couldn't find it in me to be irritated at his condescension when he was right for once. "I hate to eat and run, but I have a quick catch-up session with the social media team."

"Don't let me stop you. And son," he added on my way out. "Be sure to give Ivy my thanks. She's doing great work."

"I will." Another strange thing. Last week at this time, I would have gone burning hot and boiled with resentment if I heard him say that. Maybe it was seeing the results of her expertise at work that helped me get over those early issues.

Or maybe it was her.

The woman herself. I found her at her desk, but instead of sitting behind her computer and typing furiously, she was giggling with a few of the other women while they drank iced coffee. She made it look effortless, getting along with everybody and relating to them instead of sitting at her desk, acting like her time was too important to be bothered with trivial things. Was that a skill she could teach me, or was it innate?

She didn't notice me at first, giving me a chance to admire her beauty without her awareness. Her glowing skin, a smile that lit up the room. Her throaty laughter had me grinning by the time I closed in on them. "Good morning," I greeted, my gaze lingering on her a bit longer than the others.

"Good morning, Mr. Diamond," one of the women chirped.

"Come on, now. It's Lucian." I turned to Ivy, who was now chewing her lip like she was nervous. "I shared the latest analytics with the big guy, and he's very impressed. Let's take five minutes after the social media team meeting to catch up."

"Sure thing." She was a good actress. No one would know she held onto the back of my head while I buried my face in her pussy over the weekend. I was twitching in my shorts by the time I reached my desk, where I had to push those memories aside to prepare for the meeting. If I couldn't compartmentalize what was becoming an obsession, I didn't have a chance of succeeding around here.

What a shame I could barely keep my thoughts off Ivy long enough to get my shit together. We had kept it professional since the weekend at her insistence. I could play the game her way for a while if it meant that much to her.

Though I hoped she didn't expect me to be a good boy indefinitely.

I should have been paying attention to social media best practices during the team meeting, but nothing interested me more than the same vanilla citrus perfume that had lingered on the pillows in our hotel room. She wore it now, the light scent playing on my senses while we sat side by side. I would never be able to smell it again without flashing back to that night. The thrill of breaking down her resistance. How she begged for me.

I shouldn't, but I had to. Some things couldn't be resisted, like the urge to nudge her thigh with mine under the table. She didn't react at first, so I did it again, a bit more forcefully this time. No way could I be the only one almost panting, needing the reminder of our connection.

Still, she refused to respond. Only when I ran the side of my foot up her calf did she gasp, then covered it with a cough. I barely bit back a triumphant grin while she continued on with the next item on the agenda.

Note to self. Tell her to change perfumes if she expects us to ever get work done.

As the meeting finished, I turned to her, my need driving me. "I was hoping we could talk a little more about the headlines we're using. There were a couple earlier this week that came a little close to clickbait for my taste."

"By all means. Let's talk about it." Did she suspect my ulterior motives? She didn't seem to, gathering her things and leading me out of the conference room without so much as a backward glance to tell me she understood where I was going with this. I didn't give a shit about clickbait and had made that up on the spot for an excuse to be near her.

When we reached my office, I had her close the door while I went to the desk and pressed the button to frost the glass and hide us from everyone else. "Hold on," she murmured, shaking her head but wearing a little grin. "What do you think you're doing?"

Admiring the way her sky-blue pantsuit accentuated her tight body and made her gray eyes look almost blue. "Giving us a little privacy so we can have a meeting, Poison," I replied, rounding the desk and coming to a stop behind my high-backed chair.

"This isn't supposed to be a meeting." She set her tablet and notepad on my desk, folding her arms while wearing a disapproving expression probably intended to chastise me. "What do you think you're doing?"

"There's a lot of things I want to do now that you mention it."

"This is dangerously close to workplace harassment. You know that, right?"

"Try to say that without smiling the way you are, and I might actually believe you." I jerked my chin toward my MacBook sitting open on the desk. "And for your information, I pulled up the posts in question. I wanted you to take a look at them and get your advice on my gut reaction."

Swiveling the chair around, I gestured for her to have a seat. "Really. Take a look."

She arched an eyebrow, eyes narrowed, but slowly walked around and lowered herself into the chair. Once she pulled up to the computer, I stood beside her, staring down her blouse while she reviewed what I had left on the screen.

"You smell incredible, Poison," I whispered, leaning down, letting my nose brush her ear. Her only reaction was a shiver.

Everything about her fascinated me, drew me in, and made me want more. Her glistening hair pulled back in a bun at the nape of her neck. Her smooth, almost glowing skin. The hint of visible cleavage when I looked down her blouse again. I was only human, and I had been a good boy all this time, including the ride back from the Catskills on Sunday. I hadn't suggested she come back to my place, though I wanted to. I respected her wishes. *"We have to be careful. Don't assume this is ever going to happen again. This can't be a thing, Lucian. It's too complicated."*

There were limits to my strength.

"I see what you mean." She turned her face toward mine, and my gaze fell to her mouth. It would've taken nothing to kiss her and taste those sweet lips. Time stretched between us until she blinked and cleared her throat, then glanced back toward the screen. "Users are savvy. They won't fall for blatant clickbait. I'll need to send the links out to the rest of the team so they can see the direct correlation between this kind of language and poor performance."

"I agree. Though I'll send it to the team."

"Have it your way." A brief smile passed over her glossy lips. "Good job identifying this."

"Thank you." I leaned in again, breathing deep, this time tracing the line of her jaw with my mouth. A feather-light touch, no pressure at all, but a moan stirred in her throat. "Since I've been such a good boy, do I get a reward?"

"Lucian, we talked about this." She was only resisting on principle, not because she wanted to. I heard the weakness in her voice.

"About me putting my hand down your pants and touching you? Did we talk about that?" My hand grazed her thigh, creeping higher. Her frustrated little groan only egged me on.

"It's been days. I just need a fix."

"Don't you have a shower in that fancy private bathroom?" She nodded toward the room in question. "Maybe you should step inside and turn on the cold tap."

"Only if you join me."

"You're the worst," she concluded with a sigh. "But no,

thank you. Maybe some other time when we aren't in the middle of the workday."

"You're not a lot of fun." I groaned and pouted when she got out of the chair, straightening her suit but wearing a coy grin. The little tease. She loved knowing how she turned me on.

Eyes twinkling, she replied, "I think we both know that's not true."

"You've got me there." I took a seat, groaning at the pressure behind my zipper. "But I think I fucked myself over."

She glanced down at my bulge, arching an eyebrow. "I am not sucking you off at your desk," she whispered. "So don't bother asking. You're the one who got yourself in that position."

A sharp knock on the glass brought an end to all of this. "Lucian? I only need a minute."

Dad.

Fuck.

Ivy's eyes bulged as she scrambled to pick up her notepad. I pulled the chair closer to the desk, hiding the erection tenting my pants.

The door opened before I had a chance to say a word, and Dad came striding in. "Oh. Excuse me." He offered Ivy a smile which she returned. "I didn't mean to interrupt."

Then why did you walk in? "We were only going over a few things from last week. What can I do for you?" I asked Dad while Ivy pretended to take notes.

"I wanted to let you know your mom insists on getting together for dinner on Friday night. I would have sent you a text, but this way, you can't pretend you didn't get the message." Dad winked at Ivy. "Not that he would ever do such a thing."

"I'll make sure there's room in my schedule," I promised. He really needed to get out of here.

"I have meetings in Philadelphia and will be there through tomorrow. See you on Friday." He made a quick exit, and I sank back in the chair, blowing out a sigh of relief.

Ivy was trembling as she dropped into one of the chairs across from me. "That was too close. What if I hadn't stopped you? He could've walked straight in on us."

"He didn't."

"But he could have," she whispered. "That's why I didn't want to do this here. I told you…"

"Enough of what you told me." I stood, rounding the desk, coming to a stop in front of her. The erection had started to go down, so she wasn't staring straight at my jutting cock. I was too concerned about the blank fear in her eyes and the tremor in her voice to continue this game. She had more to lose than I did.

"But you are right," I decided. "We shouldn't do this here."

She was too smart to take that at face value. Folding her arms, she asked, "What are you suggesting?"

"I'm not suggesting a thing, Poison. I'm telling you you're coming to my apartment tomorrow night. I would say tonight, but I have plans, though you could come along," I suggested without thinking. "You're friends with Rose, right? She'll be there."

"No, I don't think so. But thank you."

She was doing me a favor by turning me down. I was so desperate to be with her that I would have suggested anything so long as it meant being together. I was becoming addicted to everything about her, mind and body, and enough was never enough.

I was wading through dangerous shit, in other words.

"Tomorrow night. My apartment. You'll find my address in the employee files." I inclined my head toward the door. "I'm sure you have plenty to do now. I won't keep you from it."

She eyed me warily as she stood, heading to the door. She would show up. I had no doubt. She might fight with herself, but part of her was smart enough to know she couldn't deny the obvious.

There was no staying away from each other.

12

IVY

I wasn't doing this.

I wasn't actually considering this, was I?

So why was I checking myself out in front of the mirror in the bedroom section of my studio apartment? It was also the living room, considering I couldn't fit more than a bed and a single armchair in the entire room. I ran my hands down the front of my sleeveless blouse, which I bought with my first new paycheck.

Most of my increased salary had to go to Mom, but there was enough for me to buy a few little things for myself. It was cute, the flowing blue fabric skimming my hips. Paired with a pair of jeans and sandals, I could have been on my way out for drinks with friends instead of whatever the hell this was.

A booty call. Call it what it is.

And it wasn't like I hadn't chosen my prettiest bra and panties for the occasion after taking an 'everything' shower, where I shaved, scrubbed, and exfoliated every inch of my body. My carefully blown-out hair hung in loose waves that would probably fall as soon as I stepped into the humid night.

What was I thinking? I had so much riding on this job. A framed photo of Mom and me at my graduation hung close to where the mirror was mounted on the wall. I stared at it while beating myself up for being so easy. If anybody found out I was sleeping with Lucian, it would be my head on the chopping block. Men could get away with things like that, especially men in his position. Word might get around, and I could kiss my professional credibility goodbye.

Did that stop me from double-checking my purse and dropping my phone inside before checking for my keys? I made sure the tiny stove was off, turning out the lights in an apartment that was smaller than Lucian's office. It wasn't much, but it was mine, and I was actively jeopardizing it by leaving and heading outside to meet my Uber driver.

I didn't feel like dealing with the subway into Manhattan.

Upon exiting the building, a man in a dark suit called out to me from the curb. "Excuse me, Miss?"

I would normally have ignored some random creep, but the fact that he stood beside a sleek, black car that looked way too fancy for this neighborhood made me pause. "Yes?"

"Miss Ivy St. James?"

This was too weird. "That's right."

"Mr. Diamond sent me to pick you up." He stepped aside after opening the back door. "To ensure your safety."

My apprehension melted along with some of my nerves. The man was slick. I had to give him that much. Doing everything he could to get me to his apartment, even though I hadn't confirmed I'd accept his invitation. I swallowed down the fluttering in my stomach at the gesture. "Thank you," I murmured, offering a nervous smile and sliding into the back seat. It smelled brand new, and the leather was like butter.

Here goes nothing. I canceled my Uber and settled back with my heart fluttering.

The whole way across the bridge, I tapped my fingers against my bouncing knee. Along with my apprehension was a healthy dose of excitement. Anticipation. His touch—just thinking about it made my breath catch. We would have the whole night together, nobody interrupting us.

I was still caught between being disappointed with myself and counting the seconds until I got up to Lucian's apartment by the time I climbed out of the car and up to the revolving door leading into a very big, fancy-looking lobby.

What would it be like, crossing the marble floor every day, taking an elevator up to my apartment instead of walking up three flights through a narrow stairwell that always stank like mouse piss? To feel safe? Hell, when was the last time I wasn't afraid of something? Someone breaking in or following me inside and forcing their way through the door, stealing what little I had. All kinds of terrible things went through my head while I tried to fall asleep at night with a wailing baby on the other side of the thin wall separating my apartment from the one next to it.

When the elevator doors opened on the top floor, there was nothing but quiet. It was almost eerie. Lucian's door sat directly in front of me, and my heart lodged itself in my throat before I forced myself into the hallway and blew out a deep breath. Running a shaking hand over my hair, I checked in with myself again. Was this worth it? Nothing was stopping me from turning around.

My heart seized when the lock clicked, and, to my surprise, the door swung open to reveal a smirking Lucian.

So much for making a quick escape. "How did you know I was out here?" I asked.

"My spidey sense was tingling, telling me there's a gorgeous woman outside my door." He pointed up to the corner of the door frame, where a small camera was mounted. "Turns out, even an expensive security camera can't come close to displaying your beauty. Come in so I can get a better look, Poison."

He was still dressed in his work clothes, though he had taken off his tie and popped the top two buttons of his striped shirt. The expanse of tanned chest left exposed set off a familiar fluttering in my belly as I stepped inside the apartment.

"Wow." The only thing that could have stolen my attention from his chest was the apartment he led me into. This was how he lived?

It was a palace. Sleek, modern, but not cold or sterile. There was a warmth here, dark woods, leather furniture, and a fireplace that would have made for a romantic night in colder weather. I could imagine—*no, don't even go there.* I tried to focus on something else like the high ceilings and enormous windows overlooking the Upper East Side. "It's like you're on top of the world up here," I marveled. Was I whispering? I sort of felt like I should.

"It feels that way sometimes." He crossed the living room, heading for a bar set up in one corner. I noticed the photos on the walls, particularly one of him and Connor. The woman with them had to be his mother, a beautiful brunette with a mega smile which I now remembered from Rose's wedding. She had absolutely torn up the dance floor.

He noticed me admiring the photo and chuckled. "The three of us. Can I get you something to drink?"

I would need one. Something to ease my nerves. "Vodka tonic?" I suggested.

"A twist of lime?" he offered, and I nodded.

There were other photos and mementos. A lot of the same people in the pictures. "Your family?" I asked as he fixed my drink.

"Some of them. We're all pretty close, me and my cousins."

"That's right. Rose married your cousin, Colton. I forgot you were related."

"Correct." He brought me my drink, carrying a glass of whiskey in his other hand. "What about you? Is it just you and your mom?"

Somehow, I was surprised he remembered anything about me as he handed me the glass, but it was wiped away when his fingers grazed mine and set off a chain reaction of goose bumps, tightening nipples, and a shiver down my spine.

Taking a few sips of my drink, I nodded and tried to pretend I wasn't drinking the smoothest vodka that had ever crossed my lips. "Just us. She was an only child, and my dad... I don't know him. I could have half a dozen half-siblings and fifteen cousins, but I would never know."

"You could find out."

"I have everything I need." Taking another sip, I turned away from the photos to admire the rest of the grandeur around me. The floors were actual wood, not some cheap laminate. From here, I could see into the kitchen with its quartz countertops and stainless steel appliances. "A six-burner gas range?" I whispered, thinking about the tiny four-burner electric antique in my apartment. There were times I was afraid to use it.

"Do you like to cook?" he asked, seemingly genuinely interested in me.

"I love it. But I don't get much of a chance." Not to mention, most of the time, ramen noodles and cereal comprised my diet. Some months, almost everything had to go to the nursing home.

"Why do you look sad?" He touched the hand to my bare shoulder, and it was warm. Comforting.

"Do I?" I forced a laugh as I turned to him. "I don't mean to. This is all a little overwhelming."

He fell back a step, frowning. Probably upset I didn't walk in, drop my jeans, and beg him to put his dick in me. "Come, sit down," he offered, gesturing toward the black leather sofa. "I was going to put on some music. It might relax you."

"Sure, whatever you want." It was his place, after all, and he was only trying to set the mood. This was all wrong. I was fucking it up.

Soon, soft jazz filled the air. "Nice choice," I decided, smiling in appreciation, looking around to find the speakers discreetly mounted in the corners of the large room. The acoustics were incredible.

"I'm not just some uncultured swine," he pointed out with an easy grin that was so sexy. There was nothing hotter than a man comfortable in his skin, in his surroundings. A body like his didn't hurt, either.

"So you like jazz, you have tons of family photos around the apartment, which tells me family means a lot to you. You shoot a mean game of pool. You're full of surprises, Lucian Diamond."

He sat at the other end of the sofa, angling his body until he faced me. My heart skipped a beat when our eyes met, and his twinkled when he smiled. "What's on your mind, Poison?"

Now, I felt stupid for revealing what was going on in my messed-up brain. "It's nothing. I shouldn't have said anything."

"No, really. Is there something wrong with your mom? You can tell me. I would like to know more about her," he added with a soft, inviting smile. "I mean, you already know my dad personally. It only seems fair."

What was this all about? Suddenly, he was thoughtful, almost caring. Not that I didn't think he had it in him somewhere, but for someone who tended to bulldoze his way through uncomfortable situations, this came as a surprise. "She's as good as she can be. It's more like… I feel sort of lost here in this huge apartment. It's stupid."

"It isn't stupid. But you're here because I want you to be, and you want to be. There's nothing wrong with that, is there?"

"No, of course not. I just feel a little… uncomfortable, I guess. What could you possibly want with me when you have all of this?"

"Back up." He set his glass down on the coffee table, turning his full attention toward me. "Is it a bad thing that I live in a penthouse?"

"You know it isn't. But I live in a freaking shoebox compared to this. You probably have a hundred women you could be with right this minute who are more used to all of this. I'm afraid to get comfortable, like I'll ruin something."

"What are you talking about? Where is this coming from?" He laughed, but it was a disbelieving sound. "Since when are *you* so unsure of yourself?"

Since I walked in here, and the blatant difference between us smacked me in the face hard enough to sting. I couldn't bring myself to explain that. Neither of us had the time to delve through my insecurities. "There's more to me than meets the eye, I guess." It was lame and awkward, but it was the safest response.

"I doubt you could ruin anything, and if you did—" His mouth snapped shut, but it was too late. I knew exactly what he was going to say.

"If I did, you could just replace whatever it is," I finished for him.

"Jesus, Poison, relax. Enjoy your drink, listen to some music, unwind with me." There was hunger in his gaze when he looked me up and down. "You look beautiful tonight."

"Thank you." Now my new top felt cheap. I was too deep in my own head. I was ruining everything, all because I couldn't get over his obvious wealth compared to my complete poverty.

"You smell nice too, but then, you always do." He reached out and ran the backs of his fingers down my arm, leaving a trail of goose bumps in his wake. "Come closer, I won't bite. I've been looking forward to this all day."

"Me too," I admitted. If only we hadn't met here. We could've gotten a hotel room and would have been tangled up in each other this very minute. It was different when we met in neutral territory. All I could think about now was how much leverage he had over me and how miserable life would be if anybody found out about us.

"I'm sorry." I bolted back the rest of my drink and scrambled to my feet. "I shouldn't have come here. You didn't do anything wrong," I assured him as I grabbed my purse.

He stood, moving toward me. "Wait. You're not going anywhere."

"I am. I have to." I hurried across the room and headed

for the front door that marked my salvation. He was so wealthy he could have or do anything he wanted. It didn't matter to him whether I kept my job or not, just like he didn't have to work a day in his life. We were not the same.

"Why? Just tell me why, dammit," he demanded, his deep voice firmer than usual.

"Because I have much more at stake than you do, that's why. Don't pretend otherwise. Thank you for the drink, and I'll see you in the office."

"Stay." Just as I reached for the door, he took my shoulders in his big hands, pressing his fingers into my muscles. I closed my eyes, fighting the desire to melt against him and forget everything.

"I really can't, and I shouldn't." When I opened the door, his hands fell away. He didn't try to stop me this time as I left with tears in my eyes and a burning ache in my chest.

It was the right thing to do.

It was the only choice I could make.

What a shame it hurt so much.

13

LUCIAN

"Your dad tells me things are going really well at work." Mom was almost beaming across the table as she reached out to grab hold of her wine glass. "I'm so glad. I knew with a little guidance, you would kick ass at this job."

"Thanks." There was a reason I always got along better with her than with Dad. We had the same communication style.

"The analytics are impressive." Dad lifted his glass to me at the round corner table where we sat enjoying our pre-dinner drinks on Friday night. I was thinking about meeting Noah and Marcus for a drink later, but there was plenty of time to catch up with my parents. For some reason, they seemed to think it was important.

"I didn't do it all by myself," I reminded them. "I have learned a lot over the past several weeks."

"I know the family legacy will be in good hands." Mom exchanged a loving look with Dad while my insides went cold. I had no choice. My life's path had been laid out for me all because my last name was Diamond.

The funny part was I didn't hate my job. Far from it. Research and analyzing data was where I thrived—what made our readers click a link and figuring out their thought patterns. I liked it. I wanted a choice and the chance to choose for myself.

Another gulp from my glass of scotch eased some of the frustration brewing in my chest. It started building last night when Ivy decided she couldn't stand to be in my presence any longer. Since when was having money a crime? I wasn't hung up on it any more than I was hung up on her not having anything. Why was it such a big deal? Why couldn't she stick around and explain herself? It was the first time a woman had ever walked out of my apartment.

I needed to know why and couldn't trust her to tell me. But it wasn't my style to hold onto a woman who wanted to go, but I wished I had.

"I'm starving," I announced since it was better to think about that than to reflect on my Ivy situation.

"We can order in another few minutes. I would like to finish my drink." As Dad spoke, I noticed he glanced over my shoulder. He was looking for someone. This wasn't the first time I had caught his attention wandering.

"What aren't you telling me?" I set my glass down, folding my hands on the table. "Who are we waiting for?"

Mom sputtered, her lashes fluttering, but Dad's sudden smile saved her from having to explain. "Clover. It's good to see you."

I stood and turned to find a cute redhead coming our way. No, she was better than cute. She was tall and lithe with a sprinkle of freckles across her nose and sparkling green eyes that lit up when they met mine. "Lucian. Your mom told my mom so much about you, and then my mom told me."

So, she was in on the joke. Thank God for that, anyway. It was one thing to be tricked into having dinner with a woman my parents approved of, but it would have been much worse if she showed up with our whole future planned out in her head.

"Nice to meet you." I shook her hand and pulled out her chair the way I was expected to. Over the top of her head, though, I firmly narrowed my eyes at my parents. If anything, I was more disappointed in myself for not seeing this coming. No wonder it was such a big deal for us to get together.

"Clover is my good friend, Felicity's daughter," Mom explained. "We've known each other for years. I think the two of you attended a few of the same birthday parties when you were kids, come to think of it."

"Oh, sure," I said, nodding. "I think I remember you. Didn't you slap a slice of birthday cake out of my hand once? You were mad because I got the piece with the extra frosting."

Clover's cheeks went red, and she covered her mouth with one slim hand. "I can't believe you remember that!"

"How could I forget? You still owe me a piece of cake." Fuck. I was flirting with the girl. It was sort of a knee-jerk reaction—beautiful girl, a nice smile, a great body. This was routine for me, breaking out the charm without thinking about it.

I was playing straight into my parents' hands.

"Clover is a former model," Mom explained. "She went back to school and is in her second year at Harvard Law."

"Honey," Dad chided with a gentle laugh. "I'm sure Clover can speak for herself."

"It's all right," Clover said with a smile. "I don't find it easy to talk about myself, so I appreciate it whenever anyone else does it for me." The girl was any parents' dream come true. And the mention of the name Felicity told me who her parents were. A wealthy investment banker and his socialite heiress wife.

In other words, she was one of us. The sort of suitable girl my parents wanted me to settle down with.

I should have wanted her, too, even if this wasn't the ideal setup. It wasn't my nature to go along with what Mom and Dad wanted for me, and dating Clover would've meant admitting they knew better than I did. That wasn't going to happen.

Especially not when Ivy filled my thoughts. She inhabited a large section of my mind. It seemed like I was always either wanting her, fucking her, or reflecting on our last time together. I'd spent most of the day at work trying to catch her eye and ask what the hell last night was all about, but she had kept herself busy and away from her desk.

"Lucian?" Dad cleared his throat, glancing toward Clover. "You were asked a question."

"I'm sorry. What was it?" I asked, turning toward her as a server handed out menus.

"I asked how you like working at your family company. It seems like it would be pretty exciting, running all those different digital imprints." She'd gotten the full rundown prior to this awkward dinner. I was the only one left in the dark.

"I'm learning a lot," I explained, and once again, Ivy's face filled my awareness. Her gray eyes and her smile, the feel of her hair, the taste of her skin. This was a problem. Being addicted to her was one thing, but I needed to be able to focus.

"And how is school treating you?" Mom asked Clover,

handing over her menu. "I understand you're near the top of your class."

"I do what I can." She had a nice personality and laugh. There wasn't anything I could find to dislike about her. Not that I was trying.

But once again, she was not my choice.

When would I get to choose?

"Excuse me. I'm sorry, I just remembered I promised to make a phone call. I won't be long." I pushed back from the table when the air in the room suddenly felt too dry and heavy for me to breathe. I was making an ass out of myself, but I wasn't the one who put me in this position. Mom and Dad sitting there staring at us, practically hanging on every word, did. Didn't they know how pathetic this was? How blatantly obvious? Clover seemed like a smart girl. What did she think about it?

I wasn't going to stay around long enough to find out. I made my way through the restaurant, which was full on a Friday evening. If I didn't get out of here soon, I would suffocate.

The warm air outside was better than what I had just left. I loosened my tie and considered walking. Just going, leaving without another word. I could always reach out to Clover and apologize. She might even understand. What I couldn't do was sit and be part of that charade a minute longer.

"What do you think you're doing?" The sound of Dad's voice behind me left my molars grinding and my blood boiling. "You left that lovely girl in there while you're standing out here doing what?"

"Believe me," I gritted out, turning around to face him. "It's much better for me to be out here. What is this, a goddamn sitcom? Mom and Dad clumsily match their kid up with some random girl who comes from the right family? Do you know how awkward this is?"

"When will you grow up?" Gone was the charming, affable guy from the restaurant. He had never existed in the first place. "This is how it's done. You're introduced to a nice girl, you get to know each other, and you realize you couldn't possibly do much better." He ended with a short shrug.

I barked out a laugh. "Thank you for your faith in me."

"Lucian. She's beautiful, she's smart, she's got a great future ahead of her. What else do you need to know?"

"Remind me again how you and Mom met." The brief flash of uncertainty that passed over his face was gratifying. I knew damn well Mom had been close friends with Dad's sister, my aunt Lourde. They hadn't been set up by their parents, even though my grandparents had certainly tried.

"That has nothing to do with this," he scoffed.

"That has everything to do with this. You can't force me into becoming involved with someone all because you think she's acceptable. I'm not going to be part of this charade."

"Just like you didn't want to be part of the family business? Yet there you are, succeeding in spite of yourself."

This time, it made sense for Ivy to come to mind. She was the reason I was succeeding. She was someone I would much rather have had dinner with, no matter how hot and smart Clover was.

"I'm leaving," I decided. "Please, tell her... I don't care what you tell her. I got called away."

"No." He tried to block me. A waste of time on a wide sidewalk with plenty of room to sidestep him. "You will not embarrass us this way."

"Considering I never asked you to set me up with her, this embarrassment is on you."

I walked away, knowing there were too many people on the street for him to try to stop me. If there was one thing Dad couldn't stand, it was making a scene. He was much too important to do anything so low class.

I walked one block, then another. My head pounded with every step I took. The bastard. What the fuck was he thinking? I would catch hell the next time I saw him, though I couldn't bring myself to care. He brought this on himself. It was bad enough I had to play along in the office.

Dad had sent a car to the office to pick me up for dinner, meaning I had to grit my teeth and order an Uber. I could have walked home if I were going there, but the last thing I felt like doing was sitting alone. I was in no mood to bullshit with the guys, either. To sit around and hear about how happy they were while my fucking parents tried to set me up tonight like I was some hopeless wreck, unable to find a woman on his own. The more I thought about it, the worse it pissed me off.

Rather than order the car to take me home, I copied and pasted an address I'd gotten from office records earlier today. On a whim, I had looked up Ivy's address to get a sense of where and how she lived.

Now, I would see with my own eyes what I had looked up online. A tiny, rundown walk-up in a shitty part of Brooklyn, where rents were cheap and crime was higher than the surrounding area. In other words, something she could afford on the pittance she'd probably made at Jones. I didn't know if she would be home, but I wanted to try.

Once we were on our way, I tried to call her. The phone rang several times before sending me to voicemail. She probably had a life. Work could not be all there was. I ended the call without leaving a message. "What am I thinking?" I muttered, staring at the phone.

"What's that?" the driver asked, raising his voice to be heard over his shitty music.

"Can I change the destination? I've changed my mind." Instead, I sent him to the bar, where Miles and Noah told me to meet them after dinner. Fuck it. I wasn't going to show up on some woman's doorstep, and I wasn't going to sit around feeling sorry for myself. I was Lucian-fucking-Diamond. While my father might not have thought much of that, I had stopped listening to his opinion years ago.

There was only one person whose opinion seemed to matter at the moment, and she didn't want me.

14

IVY

It took literally everything I had to drag myself up the stairs on my way to my apartment. I never thought I'd look forward to seeing it the way I did late Sunday afternoon. The weekend was as good as over.

It was like I'd been living in an alternate reality the past couple of days as I camped out in Mom's room at the nursing home. It was all I could think to do once I'd gotten the call after work on Friday night, telling me she fell again. This time at the expense of her hip.

Just thinking about it made emotions swell in my chest, threatening to crush me. I couldn't let it upset me again. I'd spent the whole weekend beside myself as it was. I didn't know if there was enough moisture left in my body to shed a tear.

Did I have the fortitude to handle this? I didn't have the first clue. A long, hot shower might help put things into perspective, not to mention at least eight hours of sleep. Maybe more. My level of exhaustion left me considering crawling into bed and sleeping until morning. Just then, I felt like I could pull that off easily.

What was I going to do? They weren't taking care of her, not as well as they should've been. "*I had to go so badly.*" I could hear Mom's voice in my head. The tremor in it, the embarrassed tears when she had to admit she couldn't do something as simple as get herself to the bathroom without falling. "*I pressed the call button so many times, but nobody came. I didn't want to wet the bed and lie around in it.*"

There wasn't much I could say. I couldn't exactly get on her case because she needed to use the bathroom. When I asked for answers from the staff, all I got was the same excuse. They were understaffed, they were doing the best they could, there were too many people in too many beds, and besides, they couldn't come running for every little thing.

That choice of words still boiled my blood hours after hearing them. *Couldn't come running for every little thing.* What was the point of a patient being there, then? That was what I would have asked, too, if I wasn't so concerned about alienating the people in charge of keeping Mom safe. Then again, they weren't keeping her safe, were they? Twice in one week, she felt compelled to get up and do something on her own because no one would help her. I asked myself again, *What was the point of them?*

Did it matter? The fact was, I didn't have enough money put aside yet to afford anything better. Even when I scrimped and saved every spare penny, it wasn't enough. I didn't know when it would be. This was the best I could do for the time being.

I never felt so lost and hopeless. What was the point of anything?

In other words, I was in a low, dark place by the time I reached my front door and slid the key into one lock, then the second. I had packed a bag, so at least I was able to change my clothes while I was there, but I felt soiled and sticky after going two days without a shower.

I wasted no time after locking the door, kicking off my shoes, and taking off my clothes on the way to the bathroom. Not that it was a very long walk.

The first touch of steaming water against my skin was almost good enough to bring tears to my eyes. It took a situation like the one I'd faced over the weekend to remind me of the simple pleasures in life and how lucky I was to have them. Crossing my arms against the tile wall, I touched my forehead to them, letting the water run over my shoulders and back in an attempt to loosen them. They had been tight for days, and sleeping on a rock-hard couch all weekend played a big part.

By the time I left the shower after washing my hair three times to get rid of the odor that had soaked in—stale, sour, nasty—I slipped my robe on and wrapped a towel around my dripping hair. Somehow, it felt easier to face the world now, and Lord knew I needed all the help I could get. What did I need to do? How could I help her?

She wasn't my only problem, either. I had kept my phone on silent over the weekend, wanting to give Mom a little peace and quiet where possible, but that didn't mean I had missed the phone calls from Lucian. What was up his ass all of a sudden? He never left voicemails, either, so I had no idea why he was calling. Looking for a good time, maybe? If so, I was not the girl he wanted to talk to because I would not be a good time for anybody.

Now, pulling the phone from my bag, I found a new missed call had come in while I was scrubbing the pee smell out of my hair. Once again, no message. I shook my head with a sinking heart. Knowing him, all he wanted was to know why he couldn't get his dick wet last week. To him, that was the biggest concern he had. He lived a charmed life otherwise.

One he decided to make my problem when out of nowhere, his voice rang out on the other side of my front door not three seconds after I sat on the bed. "Poison? I hear you in there. Open up." He paired that with another knock, louder this time.

He had to be kidding, right? He wasn't seriously here, disturbing what little peace I had left.

Maybe if I didn't say anything, he'd give up. I picked up my phone and went back through my list of voicemails, but none of them were from him, and he never sent a text to tell me what was so important.

"I want to make sure you're all right," he called out. "You're too type-A to go a whole weekend without returning a call. Let me know you're okay."

This was strange, even for him. So much so it got me off the bed and across the living room. I flipped open the chain across the door before opening it to find him scowling. "Finally," he grunted out. "This is what it takes? I have to come all this way and make a goddamn jackass out of myself to get a response out of you?"

He looked good, but then he always did, though his scruffy cheeks and tousled hair weren't nearly as important as the arrogant look he wore. "First of all, what gives you the right to demand a response in the first place?" I snapped. Was he serious? "Secondly, if it was so important to speak to me, why didn't you leave a message and let me know what was on your mind? Am I a mind reader now?"

He probably wasn't expecting me to spout off on him by the way his mouth fell open, his brows lifting in what looked like surprise. "I only wanted—"

"You only wanted what?" I asked, cutting him off before

he could continue pissing me off. "I hate to tell you this, but I'm not some chick you can call up at all hours whenever there's an itch in your pants. I have a life. And I don't owe you anything."

"Maybe cut the nasty attitude, Poison," he suggested, eyes going narrow. "I didn't have to come all the way over here to make sure you were alive."

"Oh, is that what you were doing?" I asked with a disbelieving laugh. "Thank you so much. Now, if you wouldn't mind, I would like to enjoy what is left of my weekend in peace."

He craned his neck to look past me at the bag behind me, left on the floor, along with the T-shirt I was wearing when I got home. "Where were you?"

"Is there a problem with your hearing?" I genuinely could not believe this. "Where do you get off? If you had come here genuinely asking the way a friend would ask another friend if everything's okay, that would be one thing. But no, you show up with this weird, possessive attitude and demand information. I've been through enough lately, all right? I don't have it in me to handle you too."

I tried to close the door, but of course, the idiot was too quick for me, placing his hand against it. It was irritating how little effort it seemed to take for him to deny me. "What have you been through?"

"Stop—"

"I'm asking as a friend, like you said. What have you been through? What happened? Talk to me, Poison," he urged. "I'm already here, so you might as well do it."

"You are so goddamn charming when you feel like it." I was too tired to fight anymore, so I let go of the door and allowed him in. "I've had a really terrible weekend. I've had a terrible, oh, nine months, come to think of it. But this weekend topped them all."

"How?" He came in, sizing up the room with a single glance, and I couldn't help but remember how my apartment compared to his. Why did I let him in? What must he be thinking?

I swallowed back the flash of shame that raced through me before I could help it. There were no explanations needed, not to him or anybody else. I did the best I could with what I had.

But it wasn't enough. It never would be because I wasn't enough.

Without thinking, I dropped onto the bed and covered my face with my hands. "It's all hopeless. There's nothing I can do. I'm so lost."

Somewhere in there, he dropped to his knees, gently pulling my hands from my face so I could look at him through eyes blurred with tears. "Talk to me, Poison. Are you all right? Are you hurt?"

"Mom is…" I blubbered. "She broke her hip. I was with her all weekend, and I'm fucking exhausted, and I don't know what to do for her."

A long breath escaped him. "Oh, Christ."

Now that I had opened the floodgates, everything came pouring out. I'd been holding it all inside for so long. "They're not taking good care of her there. She needs more attention than they can give her, but I can't afford that. Look where I live!" I barked out a high-pitched laugh, sweeping an arm around. "This is my palace. This is all I can afford after paying for her expenses. And it's not enough. It's still not enough."

His mouth worked like he wanted to offer something but didn't have the first clue what. No big shock there. No doubt, his biggest worry normally had to do with not getting a reservation at the hottest new restaurant. Eventually, he pulled himself together enough to offer, "I'm sorry you're going through this. I'm sorry she is... I... wish I knew what else I could say." Through my blurred vision, I noticed the way his eyes lit up. "Let me help. I want to help."

Red flags waved frantically in my head. "No. I couldn't let you do that."

"Don't let your pride get in the way now, Poison," he scoffed. "This is important. You know I have more than enough—"

I didn't need to hear this. "I know you do, but I can't accept it."

"Why won't you let me help? If not for yourself, for her."

He had no idea how he was twisting me up inside. Because he had a point— he would never miss the kind of money it would take to have Mom in a nice place with nice people, somewhere she could recover and make friends. That was all I wanted for her.

But what would it cost? Because money wasn't the only thing in question here. What would I owe him beyond dollars and cents if I let him take this step? It would connect us in a way I wasn't sure I wanted to be, no matter how good he was in bed or how much I appreciated the concern he showed.

"Because some things... I just can't do," I concluded with a shrug, sniffling as the wave of emotion died down. "But thank you. I mean it. You don't have to care, so it's nice to know that you do."

He sat back on his calves, scowling. "You're impossible."

"Tell me something I don't know."

When he took my face in his hands and stroked my cheeks with his thumbs, I could close my eyes and, for the first time in days—months, who was I kidding— let go. I wasn't handing him all of my problems, but I could let him bear them for a little while. Just long enough for me to release some of the tension still knotting my muscles and making my head pound. Little by little, he eased that tension, allowing me to melt into his touch.

"I'm here." His lips brushed my forehead and nose then moved down to touch my lips. "I'm right here. You don't have to be alone."

Those were the magic words. He couldn't have said anything else that would impact me as deeply. I had been so alone all these months, scrambling around, trying to take care of Mom, trying to take care of my own life or what little of it there was after I gave everything to her. I wasn't alone anymore.

He kissed me again, and this time, I kissed him back, stroking his tongue with mine, faintly moaning when he growled and pulled me tight against him, wrapping me in his arms and holding me against his firm chest. This was all I needed—to let go, if only for now and remember there was still something in my life that had nothing to do with nursing homes, hospitals, and bills.

He tugged the belt on my robe, letting it fall open, his fingertips stroking my bare skin. All at once, my sadness turned to heat, and everything that seemed so gray and hopeless burst to life in full color. All because of the way Lucian's hands slid over my skin, lighting me up and bringing me back to life.

"You are so beautiful." There was hunger in his voice, the sort that made me want him more than ever.

"Touch me," I whispered into his mouth, kissing him again. "Please. Make me feel good."

He eased me back, spreading the robe open as he did.

There was nothing in the world but sensation and pleasure. The delicious tingle left behind every time his lips touched my skin, the friction from the scruff on his cheeks chafing my thighs and my stomach as he worked his way up my body.

By the time he reached my breasts, I had to touch him, my fingers running through his hair, over his back and shoulders. How was he so damn muscular? I was glad when he pulled his polo over his head so I could feel his skin. It was so warm and easy to scrape with my nails until he growled, nipping at my throat before lapping my skin.

"Let me take care of you." It was a combination of the words and the growl running through his voice that got my juices flowing harder than ever. I was dripping wet by the time his fingers slid over my lips, teasing my slit.

"Oh, God..." I lifted my hips, desperate for more.

"Relax. Feel it. Don't rush it." He continued the same slow torture, stroking my flesh without giving me what I needed. I couldn't breathe without whimpering, completely seized by the overwhelming need for relief from this tension.

"Let go, Poison," he murmured in my ear, and the thought was so seductive. It went deeper than the physical. I wanted to let go of everything, forget anything that wasn't this. Anything that didn't feel good.

"Oh, please," I begged, on the verge of tears. "Please, let me come! I can't stand it!"

"Sure, you can." His tongue traced my earlobe, then my jaw, traveling up and down my throat. "And when you come, it'll be incredible. Do you trust me?"

"Yes," I moaned, spreading my legs wider, fighting for the contact I needed more than anything. When I was sure I couldn't take it anymore, he slid a finger between my lips and drove it inside me. "More!" I begged, angling my hips so he could go deeper. "Lucian, Christ. Please!"

"Please, what, Poison?" he whispered in my ear, breathing hard the way I was. Even that was good. Knowing he was into it, that getting me off got him off.

"Let me come before I combust!" I would die if he didn't. I couldn't take it anymore. "You're killing me... fuck!"

"You won't die, I promise." He stroked me slowly, then he added a second finger to the first, but even that wasn't enough. Nothing was as good as the feeling of him filling me, stretching me.

Something huge was building, growing in my core. Every part of me zeroed in on that sensation, working for it, willing it to explode. "Yes, yes, more, just like that!"

"Does that feel good? Is that gonna make you come?" His voice was all that kept me tethered to the world. I focused on it while the tension built, my hips leaving the mattress once I planted my feet against it so I could grind my hips.

"Let go of it," he whispered, inviting me, nudging me closer to the edge with every breath that hit my skin. "Come for me. Let me watch you come, Poison."

When it hit, it didn't happen all at once. I was climbing a staircase, higher and higher, my mouth open as almost confused cries filled my tiny apartment. It was never like this. What was happening? I was so close, hanging on the edge, just a breath away from falling apart.

"Now," he ordered, driving his fingers deep one last time, and I shuddered, clenching around him and moaning. It went on and on, finally easing enough that I could settle back on the bed with a breathless whimper. Just when I thought it couldn't possibly get better...

It wasn't over. Through half-closed eyes, I watched him

strip down, his body glistening in the late afternoon sunlight that highlighted every ripple of his body. While I adjusted myself on the bed and slid out of my robe, he unrolled a condom over his steely cock, then climbed between my parted legs.

I pulled him down on top of me, my heart swelling as he pushed his way inside. It didn't matter how many times we did this. I couldn't get over the first rush when our bodies connected like this.

It was electric, all of it. His weight was on top of me, pressing me into the mattress. His body was between my legs, moving slowly, grinding against my clit until there was nothing I could do but drag my nails across his shoulders and moan in his ear. "You feel so good."

"So tight," he grunted out. "You're gonna make me come."

There was something erotic about listening to him lose control. His soft grunts, his quick breathing, the way his rhythm picked up speed when I linked my legs behind his ass and drew him deeper.

I felt it building in me again, bigger with every stroke, consuming more of me. "Yes... yes, Lucian..." I whispered, kissing his neck and his shoulder, anything I could touch my lips to.

"Ivy." My name was music when he rasped in my ear, dropping the nickname for once. "Ivy... fuck..."

"Come with me," I begged, meeting his strokes, losing control like he was. So close. When the tension broke, he followed, groaning in my ear as shockwaves rolled through me. It was perfect, right down to the way he collapsed against me and shuddered as if he was as depleted as I was like it was as intense for him.

I closed my eyes, soaking in the blissful afterglow.

Finally, my body was loose. All it took was two enormous orgasms delivered by the most infuriating sex god on two legs.

"Can I get you some water?" I pried my eyes open as Lucian got up and stretched, examining the scratches on his shoulders. "Fuck, you came close to drawing blood, Poison." There was a wicked twinkle in his eyes when they met mine. "You'll have to try harder next time."

Who says there will be a next time? I wanted to ask him that, but I was too exhausted to make a joke. I settled for closing my eyes and curling up on my side.

Sleep caught me before I could take a sip of water and didn't let up until well past midnight when I woke to find a text from Lucian.

Lucian: *Didn't want to wake you and know if you'd want me to stay. Went out, bought sandwiches, you were still asleep when I came back. Left yours in the fridge if you're hungry, wasn't sure which kind you'd want. Slid your keys under the door. See you tomorrow.*

Sure enough, there was a pair of keys on the floor in front of the door. He had taken them off the ring so he could slide them through one at a time—smart. I could overlook him fishing them out of my bag, especially once I found three sandwiches in the refrigerator. "Turkey, tuna, roast beef," I murmured, reading the labels out loud while my stomach growled.

I probably wouldn't be able to get back to sleep right away now that I'd slept for hours, but at least I had plenty to think about—like Lucian Diamond and who the hell he was since I couldn't make any sense of him.

15

LUCIAN

"That's right. Sandra St. James. I want a case opened, but I want it to remain anonymous as to who opened it. Somebody's got to be held responsible at that place." The last thing I needed was my family name tied up in a nursing home exposé once the advocate's office got involved.

The woman on the other end of the phone clicked her tongue, murmuring her sympathetic agreement. "This is why I do what I do, Mr. Diamond. You're right to open a case based on what you've told me. I'll pay a visit to the location this afternoon and follow up with you in the next couple of days."

I thanked her, then ended the call. Having spent time over the past week looking into what I might be able to do to help Ivy's mom, I decided this morning to officially open a case to investigate the practices in that shithole. Ivy might not want to accept my money, but I could use my influence on her behalf. It looked like I'd be able to fast-track an investigation into the facility where Sandra was being cared for.

It wasn't enough.

Fuck, how was I supposed to know Ivy's entire life was wrapped up in her mother? Idiot. You should have figured it out on your own. Here I'd been all these weeks, maybe too full of myself for taking charge of the team the way I had and feeling a little smug after earning the respect of my employees.

And it never fucking hit me that Ivy made more than enough to live in a better apartment than the shoebox she currently called home. I was never inside until I showed up unannounced, but I'd seen the building on Google Earth. I'd had a pretty good idea of what I would find once I was inside.

This wasn't enough. I had to do more for her. Why? Because this wasn't just any woman. Ivy opened my eyes to a few things I never considered. I'd never had to. Not for a day in my life had I faced the challenges Ivy took on every day. I'd never woken up and wondered if there would be a phone call telling me my loved one needed help I couldn't provide. I never had to make the choice between paying my bills and filling my refrigerator. But it was much more than that. Ivy was more to me than that.

A brief look around Ivy's apartment on Sunday night told me what that decision looked like for her. She'd passed out cold after we finished, too wiped out to do more than curl up in a ball on the bed that must have also served as a sofa and a dining table.

It had given me the chance to get to know her better. Her refrigerator held nothing more than a few cups of yogurt and half a carton of eggs. The cabinets? Packets of Ramen, boxes of instant oatmeal, and generic cereal.

There was a photo on the wall beside a full-length mirror. Ivy, several years younger, smiling wide in her cap and gown. Beside her was a woman who could easily have been an older sister. Ivy's joy had reflected on her face.

Lost in my thoughts, I turned to gaze out toward Ivy's desk. She was busy as always, going over reports with a couple of the girls from the team. No one would ever know she had all of this going on in the background of her life, and that if it wasn't for the meals provided at work, she might have gone hungry.

And she was one person. A single employee. How many others were there? Sure, we compensated everyone generously, but where did that money go? How many others had family members who needed support? How many people had to choose between medication for themselves or someone who depended on them? What the hell was I supposed to do about it?

It was almost a relief when I recognized Dad strutting down the hall, coming my way. Things hadn't exactly been warm or friendly between us since I walked out on dinner, but what else was new? He only started trying to be my friend after he shoved me into this fucking job.

Still, gritting my teeth through a talk with him was somehow easier to swallow than sitting around, thinking about Ivy's problems, wondering if there was another way I could help her without insulting her.

He barged in without knocking, but that wasn't a surprise. It wasn't like I couldn't see him coming, anyway. "To what do I owe the pleasure?" I asked, forcing a cordial greeting for the sake of the women watching from outside the room. Women who tried like hell to make it look like they weren't paying attention when it was clear they were hanging on every moment. The reason? Dad's scowl. It was clear he meant business.

"Frost the glass," he muttered out of the corner of his

mouth. So much for greetings. I did as he asked, exchanging one quick look with Ivy as I hit the button to block her from my view.

At least I could drop the act now. "What is it?" I asked, leaning back in my chair while he came to a stop in front of my desk.

"Your mother called me in tears. It turns out she had brunch with her friend Felicity this morning and the poor girl you walked out on last Friday was humiliated. You haven't yet bothered to apologize to either of us for that embarrassing tantrum you threw, by the way."

"Thank you for noticing," I gritted out, gripping the arms of my chair rather than launching myself across the desk and grabbing him by the throat. "I had no intention of apologizing. I spoke to Clover. We're fine." I narrowed my eyes when he started sputtering. What, did he think I was going to burst into tears? "And I highly doubt Clover was as humiliated as her mom says," I continued. "Did you ever think maybe her parents wanted this more than we did? You know, just like you and Mom? I'm not going to be guilted into settling down. I can't believe we're having this conversation." As a punctuation mark, I checked the time. "I have a meeting in ten minutes, so you might want to get to the point."

He jabbed a finger at me, his face slowly going from its natural, healthy tan to a telltale shade of deep, angry red. "Call your mother. Apologize. That's a start."

"I will. I've been busy."

"I need you to understand something." He drew a deep breath and released it slowly, grinding his teeth. From where I sat, I was the only one going through pain as a result of this conversation. "I am not handing my empire over to a child who would rather spend his evenings drinking and whoring around than build something lasting. That is not the sort of man who can be trusted. Do you understand?"

"I never asked you to hand your empire over to me." Rising slowly, I studied the look of blank surprise that washed over his face. Like it was unthinkable, not wanting to accept control of his precious empire. "I'm going to need you to keep that in mind the next time you threaten me and accuse me of not being the right sort of man to take over for you."

"I know I'm not hearing this." He barked out a sharp laugh. "Not standing here in a building I own. Not from my own son."

"The next time you want to offer someone a job, make sure you explain the entirety of the terms," I suggested, hitting the button to clear the glass. "Because this is the first time I'm hearing about needing to be married to the right girl if I expect to have a future here."

There was nothing he could do, not with so many people sitting outside my office. No choice but to accept what I said without arguing. It was killing him. "Call your mother," he reminded me through clenched teeth, straightening his tie and throwing his shoulders back before striding from the room.

Ignorant bastard. Stupid too. He truly thought Clover gave two shits over what happened last Friday? *"Believe me, I get it,"* she told me when I had called her last week to apologize. *"Do you want to hear a funny story? I'm already seeing somebody, but he isn't from the kind of family Mom and Dad want me involved with. So they basically pretend he doesn't exist. My mom already told your mom I would be there, so I sort of felt like I had to go through with it."*

There wasn't a parent alive who wouldn't want their daughter to marry the son of Connor Diamond. A fucking billionaire, one of the most powerful men in media. I was the only child, the heir apparent whether I liked it or not.

Movement in the corner of my eye caught my attention. Ivy was standing, picking up her tablet, ready for the team meeting. I had offered to pay for her mom's care, and she had turned me down. She was a different breed from the people I'd known all my life—social climbers, gold diggers, general trash.

Then there was this smart, beautiful, selfless woman. I honestly hadn't known there were people like her outside of fiction.

I headed out. She waited for me, tapping her nails on her tablet and chewing her lip. "That didn't look good," she fretted in a soft voice. "What happened?"

For obvious reasons, I hadn't told her about Clover. Considering Ivy had been in the middle of helping her mother through a freshly broken hip at the same time, my problems seemed small by comparison. "Talking for the sake of hearing himself," I muttered, shaking my head. "Nothing to worry about. You look gorgeous today, by the way." There was no helping it. No matter how I tried, I couldn't keep my mind away from her body, hair, and pink lips.

"Thank you," she murmured, checking me out with a quick up-and-down glance. "So do you."

"See? It's possible for me to play nice in the office. I'm not even going to say anything about how incredible your ass looks in that dress," I added as hunger threatened to unfurl in my core. The pale yellow sheath highlighted her small waist, full hips, and drool-worthy rack to perfection.

Rolling her eyes, she whispered, "I should've known."

"You love it," I told her as we fell in step on our way to the small conference room. "By the way, if you have any plans tomorrow night, cancel them. I'm taking you out." If anyone deserved a night on the town, it was her.

"Are you trying to get us in trouble by being seen together in public?" she whispered back. "Not that you'd get in trouble. I would."

"You have nothing to worry about," I assured her. Not that I gave a fuck, I didn't care the cost. I needed to spend more time with her. Besides, what were the chances in a city as big as this?

"Well... I'm free tomorrow," she concluded, trying and failing to cover up her smile. That smile stole my breath, leaving me momentarily speechless before I exhaled it away.

"Good. Look nice," I added. Raising my voice, I asked, "How did those reworded headlines treat us last week? We set up split testing, right?"

Her head bobbed as she fought back a smile. "You almost sound like you know what you're talking about," she told me, winking as we rounded the doorway and entered the conference room.

"Nobody is more surprised than I am," I admitted.

16

IVY

Was this what Cinderella felt like? If she was real, anyway, being whisked away in a carriage on her way to the ball. Only I was in a limousine instead of a carriage, and instead of a ball, we were supposed to have dinner at a three-Michelin-star Italian restaurant. I was in no way financially solvent enough to afford a meal there, and even I knew it took nothing short of an act of God to score a last-minute reservation there when waitlists were months.

If anybody could handle it, Lucian could.

I pulled a mirror from my clutch and checked the makeup I had so carefully applied, catching a slight smudge of eyeliner on the tip of my finger before holding the mirror farther away so I could fuss with my hair. Everything seemed to be in place. I wanted to look perfect, or as close to it as I could manage.

I wanted to look like the sort of woman who belonged.

Nerves gripped me, but I ignored them, looking down at the only nice black dress I owned. It was modest but sexy, with a V-neck that revealed the swells of my breasts and cut low in the back. The hem barely flirted with my knee, and I kept adjusting it as anxiety wreaked havoc on my nerves. It was just a date.

Sure, I'd been on dates in the past, but not with a man who was my boss, even if he had never actually come out and used the term. Not with the son of a billionaire. And certainly not with someone I'd ever been this attracted to. The stakes had never been higher. I still couldn't shake my fears over what might happen if anybody found out.

So why was I doing this? Sitting in the back of a limo, smirking to myself, I remembered the looks on the faces of people walking past my apartment building as I crossed the sidewalk and slid inside. Okay, so that was a lot of fun, but otherwise... why take this risk?

It was more than the sex. As amazing as it was, it wasn't enough to risk my reputation and future. Was it? What about Mom's future, which lately had overshadowed mine?

By the time we reached Greenwich Village, the answer was clear. It was in the way my heart leaped when I caught sight of Lucian waiting outside the restaurant. The smile I couldn't suppress as I looked him over. He was sophistication personified in a dark suit, one that had clearly been tailored for him, but even the best tailoring couldn't substitute for his confidence. That was what stood out the most about him. The sort of thing that couldn't be faked. He was a man on top of the world, and he knew it, and that knowledge revealed itself in his slow grin and the way he insisted on opening the door for me rather than letting the driver do it.

He extended a hand without looking in at me. This was it. After taking and releasing a deep breath, I placed my hand in his and relished the little thrill that ran through me as I stepped out.

"Wow. I mean..." Lucian's mouth hung open while his dark eyes traveled every inch of my body, "... I told you to look nice, but you look incredible, Poison."

It was completely expected and sort of adorable, the way he said that. "Hey, I only followed orders." I gently laughed while trying to ignore the thrill of his slack-jawed appreciation. All the time I spent applying my smoky makeup, blowing out my hair, and pinning it up in loose curls had been well spent. Thank you, random YouTube tutorials.

"You look very handsome..." I murmured, tucking my hand in his elbow and letting him lead me inside, tingling all over, caught up in the magic of the moment. Walking in on the arm of the most handsome man I'd ever met, who happened to think I was incredible.

This was why I took the risk. This feeling. Him. Me. The thrill, the magic.

"It smells amazing in here," I whispered as soon as we stepped inside, where the tantalizing aroma of garlic teased my empty stomach. I had been too nervous to eat and didn't want to ruin my appetite, anyway. I would never get the chance to dine here on my own, and I didn't want to waste the opportunity.

"You smell better." Leaning in, he acted like he was going to murmur in my ear but instead brushed his nose against my neck. My knees almost turned to jelly, and I had to hold onto him to keep from hitting the floor. "You'll have to let me know the perfume you use. I intend on buying you a case."

If only. I couldn't take him at his word. Even if he meant it, he could afford to live in a fantasy world where we had a future. One of us had to be realistic, and if there was one thing life had taught me to deal with, it was reality. I had no other choice.

We were led to a table near the back of the dining room, and the soft candlelight wasn't the only thing that made my heart flutter. "For me?" I asked, admiring a bouquet of white roses in the center of the table. I hadn't seen them on the other tables as we walked through the room.

"For you." He held out my chair, and I took a seat, shuddering slightly when his hand brushed my bare back and sent heat sizzling straight to my core. Everything about tonight was more intense, more special. I was like a kid on her first date, unsure of myself and giddy. I could only hope I didn't do or say anything hopelessly gauche.

Stop that. I had my shit together. I wasn't some country bumpkin, even if I had been raised pouring water into what was left in the shampoo bottle rather than buying more right away. I needed to get out of my own way and stop self-sabotaging.

"Would you like some wine?" he asked. When I nodded, Lucian ordered a bottle and then smiled at me from across the table. "Thank you for coming tonight. You look exquisite."

"You're going to give me a big ego," I joked, but he was adamant.

"If anyone ever deserved a big ego, it's you," he insisted.

When I kept waiting for the punchline, it never came. What had gotten into him? I couldn't put my finger on it. Sure, he was laying the charm on thick, but it didn't feel inauthentic. I might have been ready to swoon over how wonderful everything already was, but I could still think straight.

I knew what it sounded like when a man was throwing out pre-rehearsed lines so he could get laid later in the evening. It didn't feel that way now. I could hear the sincerity in his voice.

"I should've asked if you like Italian food," he murmured as we accepted our menus.

"Who doesn't like Italian food?" I asked with a soft giggle. "If there was only one country whose food I could eat for the rest of my life, this would be it."

"Same here." We shared a smile, and I was the first to look away before turning our attention to our choices. Everything looked so good. I finally had to force myself into a decision, so I chose braised short ribs over gnocchi, and Lucian went with seafood risotto.

"And we would like to start with a plate of antipasto," he added, lifting an eyebrow my way. That sounded good to me, though I would have said yes to just about anything. He was so freaking handsome, so charming. Would I ever have a night like this again?

"Do you come here a lot?" I asked over a rich cabernet sauvignon.

"I get around," he said with a twinkle in his eye, grinning. "This is one of my favorite spots, but I don't typically go out to dinner by myself. Normally, I'm with family."

Did he know he tended to smile when he mentioned his family? "This is going to sound funny, but that's what I envy the most about you," I admitted. "Your family. You were an only child, but you still have your cousins, your aunts, and uncles."

"I'm lucky, I know." For once, there was no humor behind his words. No joking. Only sincerity rang out in his voice, and it threatened to make me throw myself across the table and kiss his face off. This was some potent wine.

We dug into the antipasto when it arrived and while we ate, we talked about everything and nothing all at once. He liked jazz but also appreciated a range of genres. "Between you and me, I've been known to listen to show tunes from time to time," he admitted, wincing. "My mom dragged me to more shows than I can count when I was growing up. I developed an appreciation for it."

"You're so lucky," I mused, tearing at a piece of prosciutto. "But I know what you mean. My mom loves old movies. Growing up, I couldn't understand how kids my age didn't know about the movies from the thirties and forties. I guess I was kind of the weird kid when it came to that."

"Some would say weird, others cultured." He lifted his glass to me. "Here's to our parents, forcing us to be cultured." I could drink to that and laughed as I did. Nobody would believe it if I told them how much fun spending time with him could be. How normal he seemed, so far away from the imperious young prince I first met before that welcome session.

Then again, that wasn't the first time we met, was it? I wouldn't have slept with him after the wedding if he'd given me that attitude right off the bat. Somewhere inside, I had known there was more to him.

"Tell me the truth, Poison." He set down his wine glass between courses and looked at me head-on. "Do you ever want to tell people to leave you alone when they drop by your desk a hundred times a day with their piddling problems?"

I couldn't hide my disappointment. "Those problems aren't piddling to the people who have them," I reminded him. "Like Molly Kramer. She wants to go back to school, but she's a single mom who's already spread too thin. I sort of nudged her into taking online courses. I want her to succeed. I want them all to succeed."

And now I'd said too much. His expression softened as

he leaned back in his chair. "Wow. I'm sorry. That was a shitty thing for me to say."

I wouldn't disagree. There were still things he had to learn. "I don't have a family besides Mom, so I guess, in a way, they're my family. I want to take care of them. I want them to be safe in their jobs."

"They will be," he promised with a firm nod, and my heart soared. I believed him.

The restaurant was all but empty by the time we finished our cappuccinos after dessert. It didn't seem right. I would've sworn we'd only been there twenty minutes, tops. "Is it really this late?" I asked, looking around, feeling a little guilty when I noticed a cluster of servers hanging around the hostess stand, trying not to glare at us. "I'm sure these people want to go home."

Lucian lifted a hand to signal for the check and, to my surprise, gave our server his credit card without looking at the total. "You might be the most thoughtful person I've ever met, and I'm not just saying that," he offered with a wry grin. "I would've left a tip and told myself they're only doing their job."

"At least you tip. Some people don't," I pointed out. "I waited tables in college, so I guess I'm sensitive to things like that."

There was nothing to do but shiver when his hand touched my back once I stood. We shared a brief, secret smile full of the sort of intimacy that made my heart skip a beat. "You have this way of opening me up to things I never considered before, Poison," he murmured while his deep, dark eyes traveled over my face. "How do you do that?"

I didn't have the chance to reply, not that I knew what to say, as he accepted his card from the server and scrawled a tip on the receipt, handing it back over. "Thank you very much. And sorry if we held you up by sitting around for so long."

When he caught me smirking at him, he shrugged. "At least we didn't walk in five minutes before closing and demand to be served."

We were both laughing as we left. It had to be the wine I drank with dinner that made my head spin, making me lean against him just for the sake of feeling his body.

And when his hand found mine and closed around it, I would've sworn I was about to take flight. What was happening? Was this real? I almost didn't want to believe it because that would mean trusting life to not let me down yet again. A girl could only be burned so many times before she kept her hand away from the fire.

"This has been a wonderful night. Thank you so much." Instead of ducking into the limo right away, I paused, facing him. His eyes sparkled in the lights from passing traffic, pulling me in until I could drown if I were not careful. "It's been so special."

"It's no less than what you deserve." With that, he opened the back door to the limo and helped me inside, then followed. "Home," he announced to the driver.

He hadn't asked if I would come home with him, not that I was protesting. Tonight, it felt like the natural next step.

It had to be the wine working its magic because by the time he took a seat next to me, my pussy was throbbing, and the slightest touch might have made me come.

It didn't help that Lucian draped an arm over my shoulders, drawing me closer until his leathery cologne was a blanket wrapping itself around me. "Have I told you lately how beautiful you are, Poison?"

"Now that you mention it, yes... not that I'm ever going to get tired of hearing it." I turned my face toward his and inhaled the coffee lingering on his breath before he kissed me. Slowly, deeply. Thoroughly. Until I moaned softly into his mouth and twisted so my left leg could drape over his lap.

He didn't disappoint, caressing my thigh while his tongue slid against mine. My blood was on fire, setting my body ablaze. Thank God for the privacy divider between us and the driver. Lucian had already pushed me beyond my comfort zone—fooling around in the office, flirting where anybody might hear, fucking like animals the weekend of the retreat. But performing for a complete stranger who happened to be driving at the time? A girl had to set boundaries.

Those melted away once my knee brushed Lucian's erection and deepened the craving that already had me in its clutches. A wicked idea came to me. The sort of thing I would never have considered doing outside a fantasy. Somehow, Lucian made it seem normal to challenge myself this way. To slide off the seat and kneel on the floor between his legs.

"What are you up to, beautiful?" he asked, chuckling. He could pretend all he wanted to be confused, but the man didn't hesitate to slouch a little in the seat so I could access his belt and unbutton his slacks.

"Don't tell me this is the first time a woman has gone down on you," I whispered, making him laugh until the sound died when I dipped inside his boxer briefs and pulled out his thick, warm dick. It was so hard, precum was beading at the tip. He held his breath, watching me rub my thumb over that bead of moisture.

"Head in the back of a limo." He let out a low moan

when I reached out with my tongue and ran it around the ridge of his head. "Fuck, that's nice. Do that again."

I would've done anything so long as it meant hearing that helplessness in his voice. That low animal growl that told me I was taking him to the limit. It made me much more eager to please him, to make him remember how good I was at this if we ended. No, *when* we ended because we would have to.

What difference did it make how good it felt to be with him? Every minute we spent together was a mistake. We just hadn't paid for it yet. Hopefully, we wouldn't.

I didn't want to think about that anymore. Not when Lucian placed a hand against the back of my head, his fingers massaging my scalp while his hips began to move. "Fuck, yes," he grunted out, fucking my mouth in quick, shallow strokes. "Just like that, Poison."

I increased the pressure and used my tongue against the underside of his shaft. My hands slid over his abs and his chest before coming to rest on his muscular thighs.

"You like this?" he whispered. "You like being bad?" He was getting closer, his breathing quicker, his voice raspy. I moaned in response, and he sucked in a gasp. "Oh, fuck. You're gonna make me come. Faster, faster…"

I gave him what he wanted, my head bobbing, slurping sounds mixing with his heavy breathing until he thrust upward one more time, grunting loudly a second before a rush of salty warmth filled my mouth. I swallowed it back, then again, taking every drop just to prove I could. For some reason, it seemed important. I wanted him to remember this.

He was laughing softly, maybe a little bewildered, when I rose from my knees and sank into the seat, feeling triumphant and maybe a little smug. "That was unexpected," he admitted with a breathless laugh as he tucked himself into his pants again. "Appreciated, but unexpected. Just know I plan on returning the favor as soon as you get up to my place."

Leaning closer, I whispered in his ear, "Oh, I was counting on it."

17

LUCIAN

"Oh fuck. God, yes... give it to me..." Ivy's nails sank into my back, her other hand running through my wet hair. "You feel so fucking good inside me..."

I knew what she meant. It felt heavenly inside her. Better than I could ever remember feeling. I had been with so many nameless, faceless women who may as well have been from the same cookie cutter. All the same—hot and willing, but nothing special.

Not her. Not this. Moving inside her with the shower beating down on us, we were lost in each other for these last few moments before we had to break the spell that somehow wound itself around us last night at dinner.

Waking up with her this morning felt so right, and I wished we could call out and spend the day together. I didn't want it to end.

But it would, and it was about to once my balls lifted and a familiar tingle stirred at the base of my spine. "Come inside me," she moaned, moving with me. "I'm on the pill. I need to feel all of you deep inside me."

Fuck, yes. I was already close to coming when her invitation pushed me closer than ever. But I needed more. I needed to sink myself so deep she'd feel me tomorrow.

I pinned her to the tile with my body, thrusting faster, harder, determined to bury myself to the hilt and grinding that little bit more. The head of my cock nudged at her cervix, and she gasped, letting out a pleasure-filled whimper. Feeling every inch of her without any barriers was more than I could have ever fantasized about and had me rushing to the end, giving myself over to the mind-blowing sensation. She clamped down around me and shouted her release, the sound echoing off the walls and the glass door.

It was a rush, letting myself go, burying myself deep so she could milk me, and feeling every ripple with no barrier between us. I buried my face in her neck, breathing hard, coming back to my senses while she trembled and whimpered.

"I can think of worse ways to start a day." I kissed her as I withdrew, noticing the slight touch of regret when I did. What was she doing to me?

There wasn't any time to think about that. Thanks to our quickie, we were running late, not that I minded. "Don't worry," I reminded her once we finished washing up and stepped out of the stall to dry off. "I won't get mad if you're late today."

"Thanks a lot, but I won't be." Still, though she sounded confident, she frowned. "Great. I'm gonna leave here in a cocktail dress at seven-thirty in the morning. What's that going to look like?"

With a grin, I said, "It's going to look like you had a good time, Poison. I'll send you home in my car and have you dropped off at the office too."

She paused in the act of collecting her clothes. "We can't

do that. Maybe to go home, but not to go to the office. What if somebody saw?"

I doubted anyone would notice Ivy climbing out of the back of a Rolls-Royce Ghost and somehow connect her to me, but I decided to let it go. "Whatever makes you comfortable. You'd better get moving, not that I want to let you go."

There was something bittersweet about kissing her goodbye once she was dressed, her wet hair pulled back in a ponytail, and her face makeup-free, unlike last night. She would have laughed and rolled her eyes if I told her she looked better than she did when she climbed out of the limousine, but it was the truth. She had never been more beautiful.

I knew what was happening. There was no point in denying it as I shaved and got dressed. I was falling for her. It was unexpected, to say the least, and no one could've been more surprised than me. That didn't change the way I craved her day in and day out. Not her body alone, her smell, or her taste, but Ivy herself. She was poison, after all, like the strongest heroin corrupting my system. It didn't seem like I would ever shake her.

I didn't think I wanted to.

It was Wednesday morning, and there was no time to waste. I would already be a few minutes late for my breakfast meeting with Dad at eight, but it wouldn't kill him to wait. I wasn't in any hurry to see him after his performance in my office. I could only hope he had calmed down for both our sakes as I headed out to the attached garage and got behind the wheel of my spare car, a Rolls-Royce Spectre.

It took a lot to get me to drive myself anywhere when I had a perfectly good driver who needed to earn his salary, but then he was already working. And Ivy was worth it.

Goddamn, when did I fall for her? I hadn't been paying

attention, but it was getting increasingly obvious she was becoming part of me. I didn't know how to navigate this—I had never been here before. How could I know she felt the same way? Would I have to ask my cousin, Colton, for his advice, being married and on the verge of fatherhood and whatnot?

No, something tells me it's the kind of thing I'll have to figure out on my own. The thought sent chills across my skin.

A thought that was still on my mind by the time I reached Dad's office. "Thank you for keeping me waiting," he announced when I walked in.

So that was the way it would be.

"I'm eight minutes late," I pointed out, grabbing food from the tray delivered earlier. Today, it was breakfast wraps and fresh fruit. "I hope you didn't call the police to report me missing."

He grunted behind me. "All right, let's save the smart-ass comments for a day when I have the time. There's something we need to discuss this morning."

Turning, I asked, "Don't we always have things to discuss? I hope it's not about my personal life this time."

He ignored my quip. "It's time to start thinning the herd."

His choice of words made me stop halfway to the table where he waited. "Meaning?"

"Meaning, the redundancies we discussed weeks ago. I've discussed it with the heads of the other divisions, and they understand we need to make decisions on who stays and who goes. It's been long enough since the buyout for that to be established."

There went the rest of my good mood. The redundancies. Had I forgotten about them, or did I simply not want to think about them? Either way, I had lost sight of where this was going. "I see," I choked out, taking a seat and looking down at food I was suddenly not hungry enough to eat.

Was Ivy one of them? No, Dad had told me she wouldn't be. Or had he? I took my time sipping my coffee, trying to claw the memory back. Had he confirmed anything either way?

"So?" he prompted, finishing a wedge of pineapple like a man without a care in the world. "I'm going to need your list."

"My list?"

Rolling his eyes, he sighed, "Lucian. I'm not in the mood to play games. Yes, your list. You are the vice president of the digital media division. These are your people. Who can we cut free?" The nightmare got worse. When he explained it, it made sense. Of course, I would be the one to handle this. But how was I supposed to do it?

"Being a leader isn't all about being everybody's friend. There are times when decisions need to be made for the sake of the company." He softly snorted while I stared out the window, struggling to grasp what was in front of me. "Don't worry, they'll receive severance benefits. We can afford to be generous, especially considering the boom in ad revenue you've brought in."

"They brought it in," I replied without thinking. "If we've brought in this new revenue, why not expand the division to include everybody?"

Normally, his exasperated sigh would have made my blood pressure skyrocket. I was too far past the point of shock for it to register now. "Here's a business tip," he explained in his patented condescending tone. "When your revenue goes up, the idea is for profits to follow suit. What's the point of keeping everybody on the payroll indefinitely other than wasting money and drowning in inefficiency?"

I barely heard him, gazing out over the skyline but seeing none of it. Instead, I saw people laughing at the lodge, dancing during the party, chatting over coffee at Ivy's desk.

Ivy. This was going to fucking destroy her, to stand back and watch her friends being laid off with no warning. "How am I going to tell them?" I whispered, dread filling me along with a lot of guilt.

"How will you tell them... or how will you tell her?"

There was a healthy dose of suspicion in his voice, but I dismissed it. I had bigger things to worry about than his suspicious nature. What, was it that unthinkable, caring about a colleague? "I'm sure Ivy will be upset if that's who you mean."

"Upset to lose her job? I'm sure she will be."

There had been times in my life when I would have sworn my brain rebooted like a computer. When I heard something so shocking, I couldn't react or even absorb it at first—most recently when Colton announced Rose's pregnancy at their engagement party. That was a real brain reboot moment.

It was nothing compared to this, almost choking on my spit as I turned back toward Dad. He had the audacity to blink at me, blank-faced. "What?" he asked. "Obviously, she would have to go. She taught you a great deal, and she will be rewarded for it, trust me, especially because she made it possible for you to take control of your team. I'll always be grateful to her for that."

It was all wrong, but things were always going to be this way. I let myself forget, was all. Or maybe I wanted to forget. In the end, it didn't matter. I was in much too deep for this to only be a matter of business.

How could I tell him? Desperation started bubbling in

my chest. "We can't keep her on?" I asked, rubbing my sweaty palms against my thighs. "She has such a good way with people, and everyone on the team respects her."

"Are you looking for an assistant?" he asked, tipping his head to the side. "Because you will need one now that you're stepping fully into your position."

"Dad, how can we ask a former vice president to work as an assistant?"

I knew I was in trouble when he set his coffee aside and folded his hands on the table. "Why don't we get down to business?" he suggested. "I'm through fucking around with you. I know where you were last night. I know who you were with last night. And there will never be a better time to get that girl out of this company because she is not the sort of girl you need to become involved with."

For the second time in minutes, I had another brain cataclysm. Normally, I would have broken my back to hide my shock and dismay. There wasn't much I hated more than letting him know he got to me.

There was no pretending now, with the edges of my vision going red. "You would go that far to meddle in my life?"

"You think I wouldn't have you followed after your performance lately? Thumbing your nose at me, embarrassing your mother, giving our friends a reason to gossip. Do you know me at all, Lucian?"

I couldn't make sense of anything he was saying, thanks to the screaming in my head. "You followed me?"

He had to scoff, the bastard. "I had you followed. At my age, I don't have the stamina to keep up with you. I know you were out. I know who you were out with, and it's not happening. She's taught you what you needed to learn, and it's time for her to go along with the others we don't need."

And that was it. The great Connor Diamond had made up his mind. To hell with the rest of us.

"How can you do this?" I asked in disbelief.

"How can I make decisions for the best outcome of my company?"

My teeth gritted, I growled, "How can you treat people like they don't matter?"

"Oh, don't give me that." He waved a dismissive hand, scoffing. "You're only saying this to go against me."

"You would think that because you think everything I do revolves around you and our family name. Ivy cannot afford to lose this job. I am not letting her go." Was I only talking about the job? I couldn't tell. Did it matter?

He leaned back in the chair, head cocked to the side. "Are you listening to yourself? Do you know how this sounds?"

With my teeth bared in a snarl, I didn't care to hide anymore. I grunted out, "I. Am not. Letting her go."

"Then you will find a job elsewhere because we do not need her."

Was it his choice of words or the cold way he delivered them? Regardless, a switch flipped in my head. That was all it took for everything to change. "You know what? That's a great idea." I stood, buttoning my jacket. "Thank you."

"What? What's a great idea?"

"A new job. Because I want nothing to do with this one."

He clicked his tongue like he was disappointed. "All right, enough bullshit. You don't want me to call your bluff, son."

"Frankly, I wish you would. If Ivy goes, so do I. She is the only reason I've been able to do a damn thing. And as for her 'not being the right kind of woman,' " I continued, making air quotes with my fingers. "You couldn't be more wrong. At your age, shouldn't you know there's more to a person than the family they were born into? Or how much money is in their trust fund? Are you that shallow?"

The funny thing was, it hadn't been that long ago since I felt that way—considering myself better than the people working for me or laughing off the idea of sharing a hotel room with one of them, never imagining what their lives were like outside the office. Not until Ivy had opened my eyes and revealed the sort of boss *and man* I wanted to be.

It was my turn to scoff at him, backing away. "You can take this job, this company, and your goddamn precious legacy and shove them up your self-righteous ass. I'm gone."

"You are not," he insisted as I turned away, marching to the door.

"I am. I've never wanted this in the first place."

"You have a responsibility to this company as one of its vice presidents. You will not storm out of here in a huff unless you don't care about the trust fund I could easily revoke."

My trust. He was threatening my trust, cutting me off.

What a shame we hadn't stayed in bed this morning.

"What are you saying?" I asked, my back to him while I stared out at the cubicles and the people arriving for the day.

"I'm saying you will provide a list by close of business tomorrow. On it will be the names of who we're letting go at the end of the day on Friday." I didn't need to see his face to know he wore a triumphant smirk. "We already have the benefits packages put together and only need the names."

"Not Ivy," I warned. "I'm not letting her go."

His soft laughter followed me out of the room. "We'll see about that."

He had me by the balls, and there was nothing I could

do about it unless I wanted to start my life from scratch. Even without that to consider, walking out would cause an enormous scandal. As much as I would've loved to see Dad's head explode over negative press, I didn't love the idea of being hounded in the media my family didn't control. It would break Mom's heart too.

What about Ivy's heart? How could I face her now?

It was still well before nine, meaning her desk was empty. Still getting ready, probably, after ducking out of my place in last night's dress. I decided to hole up in my office, the glass frosted for privacy's sake, while I worked like hell to find a way out of this disaster.

If there was a way out.

18

IVY

Lucian had been completely unreachable on Wednesday, in his office with the glass frosted, so there was no looking inside to see what he was doing. I didn't like how worried I was about him. I heard noise coming from behind his closed door once or twice, something that sounded a lot like drawers slamming and that kind of thing.

I knew he was there.

I also knew he clearly didn't want to speak to me or to anybody. There didn't have to be anything wrong with that, did there?

Then came Thursday. He hadn't bothered coming into the office at all. All day, his desk had been empty, and he'd only offered short, flat answers to the few texts I talked myself into sending, afraid I would come off clingy or demanding.

Everything about him set off every insecurity I thought I had left behind in my teenage years. I was second-guessing myself, weighing every word, not to mention feeling less than thanks to his wealth and my definite lack thereof. All it had taken was a month of working with him and being with him to make me feel like the poor girl who never quite fit in. I didn't want to be her. I thought those days were behind me.

Yet there I was, jumping on my cell like it was a live grenade as soon as I got a text from him on Thursday afternoon. It was late, and I was about to pack it in, but he had probably predicted that based on his message.

Lucian: *Come straight to my place. I need to see you.*

It would make me the biggest loser in the world to jump as soon as he snapped his fingers and demanded my presence. Not requested, demanded. He didn't ask if I had plans. He didn't give me the chance to go home and change. I was supposed to show up because he said so.

Damn me for being a hopeless idiot, then, because instead of heading down to the subway, I grabbed a cab to his apartment. *Relax, already*. I was completely losing my grip, freshening my makeup, pulling the clip from my hair, and shaking it out over my shoulders. My hands were trembling, and my breathing was fast and shallow. I was a bit disappointed in myself for acting like such a nervous, giddy girl because a man told me to meet him at his apartment. Was that all it took? I didn't know what to think about myself.

Not that I felt like thinking about it at the moment. What if he was sick? I should've asked. I could've brought him soup or something else to help him feel better. *What is wrong with you? He is not a child. He can order his own soup.*

Shit. Had I already fallen?

The question was still rattling around in my brain by the time I stepped out of the cab and headed into his building. *Breathe, for God's sake.* I couldn't help my excitement.

Everything had seemed perfect on Wednesday morning. I had floated into work, surprised there weren't little animated birds and bunny rabbits singing to me as I walked into the office. Being pretty much ignored all day had deflated the hell out of me, and his standoffishness all day today hadn't helped. I even asked myself if I had maybe done something wrong. I was that fucked in the head when it came to him.

And there was nothing I could do about it. When I wasn't paying attention, I'd fallen for him. I was on my way to falling, at least by the time I reached the top floor, where the doors slid open and left me staring at his apartment door.

Relax. You're an adult, for Christ's sake.

I knew he could see me if he checked his security camera, but I knocked anyway, resisting the urge to fidget as I waited for him to answer the door. I looked fine.

As it turned out, I looked better than fine, at least according to Lucian, once he opened the door and took one look at me. "God, you are gorgeous, Poison." That was all he said before taking me by my arm and pulling me into the apartment, kicking the door closed while he kissed me like it was the last thing he would ever do.

At first, it was enough to let him kiss me, pushing up against the closed door, his hands running up and down my body and waking me up all over. And I asked myself, *why did I get so weird and giddy and unsure of myself when it came to him?* This was why. Because deep down inside, I didn't want to lose this. The rush, the thrill, the chemistry. It had never been like this with another man, and I couldn't imagine how it ever would.

Even so, after those first few breathless seconds, I softly laughed while he ran his lips over my throat. "What is this all about? I thought you were sick," I breathed out, moaning when he cupped my breast. "You don't feel sick right now."

"If I were sick, this is the only cure." He barely took time to come up for air, looking at me with so much fire in those endless, dark eyes. "You're the cure."

"There I was, thinking I was poison." I could laugh about it now. There were so many things I would never have imagined laughing about, but I wouldn't have imagined this, either. We had come so far.

Stop thinking like that. The man had his hand inside my shirt and his dick pressing against me, yet I still chided myself. I needed to get out of my head, or I would ruin everything, but then why had he almost ignored me for the better part of two days? There was no explanation, no nothing. He hadn't even told me why he wanted me to come over here, though this could very well have been the reason.

"Let's get rid of this," he rasped. All at once, he pulled my sleeveless blouse over my head and buried his face between my breasts, still covered in a bra I was glad I wore. "So sweet."

I closed my eyes and let myself go, let him take over. It was always so good when he did.

I squealed when he grabbed me by the hips and lifted me, pulling me in close to his erection. With my legs wrapped around his hips and my arms around his neck, I let him carry me deeper into the apartment.

There weren't many things that could pull me out of a moment like this, but my phone ringing was one of them. My heart sank as I looked over Lucian's shoulder to where I had dropped my bag on the floor. "Hang on a sec," I murmured in his ear, nipping the lobe.

"It can wait," he grunted out, walking faster, taking me to the bedroom.

"No, really. I'm sorry, but you know I can't ignore a phone call." That was the whole reason I left my ringer on in the first place, in case someone called about Mom. "Give me a sec. It's probably nothing."

He still hesitated for a moment, then placed on my feet so I could jog over to my bag and fish the phone out before the call got cut off.

"Oh. It's Laney." It was rare for her to call me, though. We usually talked at work, sometimes via text. "Sorry. I just wanna make sure everything's okay."

"Wait..." I heard the disappointment in Lucian's voice, and it seemed kind of funny from where he was a minute ago. That was what was on my mind as I answered the call.

"Hey. Everything okay?" I asked. "I'm kind of in the middle of something." I grinned at Lucian, who oddly looked like somebody had just killed his dog.

"Where are you?" she barked. "Did you know? Tell me you didn't know."

Another look at Lucian, this time searching for answers. Reassurance. Something. "Did I know what?" I asked. There was a sick feeling starting to brew in my gut, but I still didn't know why. I only knew something felt wrong.

"They're letting us go tomorrow. Maybe the whole team! Redundancies," she spat, laughing bitterly. "Can you believe this bullshit? We've only been there for a fucking month!"

"Slow down." As I spoke, I stared at Lucian, whose face was stony. "Start from the beginning. What did you hear?"

"Brad heard." Laney's voice was shaky, heavy with emotion. She had been crying. "There's a list. All the divisions have a list. They decided which ones were actually valuable to the company and who could just be let go. They're supposed to tell us about it tomorrow. He overheard it from one of the guys in marketing. All of the divisions. They didn't intend on keeping all of us. They just wanted to see who they could use, like a tryout. Maybe it would've been nice if they fucking told us," she huffed out.

"Okay, let's take a step back." Who the hell was I to talk? I was shaking, with nausea rolling over me. Everything was falling apart all at once, and there was nothing for me to do but stand back and watch it happen.

He wasn't supposed to do this.

He told *me* he wouldn't do this.

"Forget taking a step. We're done! You know, they probably didn't keep anybody. They were practically fully staffed before this fucking buyout. I knew I should've been looking for a new job all this time! What are we supposed to do?" she finished on a sob.

One thing I knew for sure. "I promise you... I didn't know about this."

"No, of course you didn't. Because they probably don't wanna keep you, either. You were there to teach the Crown Prince how to do his job, and now you can go. The heartless fucking bastards."

My God. When she put it that way, everything was so clear. All this time, I was there as a tool, nothing more. Someone to use until there was nothing left to use me for. A wave of nausea threatened to knock me down while betrayal wedged a white-hot knife in my chest. I actually looked down, expecting to see it sticking out from my chest.

Lucian turned away, rubbing the back of his neck with one hand. This explained a lot. The way he had avoided me. The way he attacked me when I first walked in here. He wanted one more screw for the road. He had to know I'd want nothing to do with him once I knew what he was doing behind my back.

"Let me call you back later tonight," I offered Laney

while my heart ached at the sound of her soft sobs. "And I promise, everything will be all right. We will all be fine."

"I really hope you're right," she mumbled miserably as I ended the call and released a long, shaky breath.

Finally, his voice broke the silence. "I can explain." That would be the first thing out of his lying mouth, wouldn't it?

I let out a faint, shaky laugh, standing near the door while he stared out the window from the center of the living room. We may as well have been miles apart when, just minutes ago, we were entangled in each other. "Please, give it a shot. I can't wait to hear it."

"I did everything I could. I spent the past two days trying to find a way to justify keeping everyone on, I swear it." He turned, and his beaten expression satisfied me for a heartbeat. "I swear to God. I don't want this."

"Why didn't you tell me? How long have you known?"

He lifted a shoulder. "Does it matter?"

He couldn't have hurt me worse if he hit me. That shrug. "Which question are you answering?"

"About how long I've known, of course." He had the nerve to act exasperated. "As for why I didn't tell you—"

"I can answer that one." I snarled. How could I ever think I was falling for him? The slimy little weasel, this cowardly little shit. "You didn't tell me because I wouldn't fuck you if I knew you were planning on letting most of the team go when you told me it wouldn't happen."

"That's not true!"

"Right. So that's why you were all over me the second I walked in here. No important talk, no sitting down with me, offering me a drink, holding my hand while you walked me through this. You wanted to fuck. After that, you could give me the news that I no longer have a fucking job." I was shaking so hard it was tough to speak, but I had to get every word out. He needed to hear it. I needed to say it.

"It's not like that!" he bellowed. "Let me get a word in edgewise, for God's sake!"

"I don't want to hear anything you have to say." I had to get out of here. I couldn't breathe. My blood was on fire, and I was a second away from throwing up all over the floor. My job. I was going to lose my job. I would have to find something else, but what if I couldn't? The market was shit. Mom needed me. *Mom.* What was going to happen to her?

"Would you please let me explain?" he asked, taking the first steps toward me. When I backed up against the door, he stopped, his hands tightening into fists at his sides. Poor baby wasn't used to being denied.

"What is there to explain?" I asked with tears in my voice. "This was how it was always going to be. Damn, how can I be so stupid?" I didn't know who I was more disappointed with. "I have to go. I can't look at you."

"Listen! I put my name down on that list, not yours." My mouth fell open, and he continued in a rush of words, "I don't want the job. The only thing that made me want it was being there with you. You'll do much better at it than I ever could. I named myself as one of the team members who had to go."

"Oh, get real," I spat. He dropped back a step, his mouth falling open. "You actually think your father would accept that? Right, like he's going to let you go and keep me, all because that's what you think should happen. You still don't get it, and you never will. You were born with a safety net. He will not desert you."

"*I'm* not deserting *you.*"

"It doesn't matter if you are or not! I'm alone either way." Saying those words had a strange effect on me. It was one thing to know something but totally different to say it out loud. "You could've told me about this. Why didn't you tell me?"

"I... I don't know." He shook his head, running a trembling hand over his hair. "I couldn't find the words. I thought once you knew I put my name on the list to keep you on, you would know I wanted to protect you."

"Nice gesture," I admitted. "But that's all it is. A gesture. It doesn't mean anything real."

"Who says?"

"I say!" Hot tears flowed freely down my cheeks, and I wiped them away, angry at them, angry at me. "You don't live in the real world. And that's why we cannot work. Do you think just because you tell Daddy you want things a certain way, that's the way they're going to be? Because that's how your life has always gone."

"And you're telling me I'm the one who doesn't understand reality when you think it's all so simple?" He barked out a cold, nasty laugh. "Is that what you think my life is?"

"I know it is! You come from this world where people are something to be used, bled dry, and tossed aside when there's nothing left. And still, somehow, you think you can make things better just because that's how you want them." Throwing my arms into the air, I concluded, "You're blind. You're blind to the way things really are, blind to the lives of the people who work for you. God, Lucian."

"That's not me anymore," he insisted with desperation in his voice. "You've changed me."

"Easy to say," I spat.

"It's true. This wasn't my idea. I wracked my brain for two days, trying to come up with a way to keep everyone on, but I'm not the CEO. He's set on what he wants, and that's it."

And this was his son, who was cut from the same cloth. Any so-called change in him wouldn't last long. I couldn't give my heart to him.

He already has it.

I couldn't look at him anymore. But turning my back hurt just as much, even if it was the right thing to do. The only thing to do. I had no business being here, no business with him. I only let myself believe it for a minute.

"Don't go." He was quick, slamming a hand against the door above my head. "Don't leave. We'll find a way through this."

"And what makes you think that?" I touched my flushed forehead to the cool wood, wanting more than anything to believe him. That was the worst part of all. How much of me still wanted to believe, to hope.

His breath stirred my hair when he replied, "Because we just have to, Poison."

"I wish I had as much faith as you. Now let me go. Please," I added when he didn't move.

"This isn't over." He stepped back, and I opened the door.

"This never began." My heart screamed out for me to take one more look at him before I left, but something told me that would be the biggest mistake of all. Because if I looked at him now, I wouldn't be able to leave. I would betray myself all over again, and I had already done enough of that.

"We'll finish this tomorrow," he told me as I stepped into the hall.

"You won't see me tomorrow. If I'm getting let go, somebody can tell me over the phone." Because, for once, I couldn't be there for my people. I couldn't walk them through this. Hell, I didn't think I would be able to stand the pain in their eyes, especially when there was more than enough pain tearing me to pieces. For once, I had to think about myself.

Besides, if I never saw Lucian Diamond again, it would be too soon.

19

LUCIAN

"I have to admit. I thought you were bluffing." The sound of Dad's voice over my shoulder didn't slow me as I packed up my office on Friday morning, early enough that I'd assumed I wouldn't cross paths with anyone. Him included.

I couldn't help but bristle and shrug, stacking framed photos in a box. I had only started adding things to the decor over the past few weeks, so there wasn't much. "You should know me better than that by now," I mumbled when it seemed like he was waiting for a response.

"I want to talk about this."

"There's nothing to say." I forced myself to turn around and face him, surprised by what looked like genuine concern wrinkling his brow. This was what it took to get through to him, to prove I meant what I said.

"Really?" He folded his arms, scowling. The angry king, dressed impeccably and groomed within an inch of his life. Yet he couldn't get his way. "What do you plan to do now? I told you you're cut off if you embarrass this family by shirking your responsibility."

"I have money in the bank. I didn't blow everything I already received from the trust, you know. I can get by for a while. Last I checked, I have a college degree and a strong network to fall back on. I'll be fine." That was nothing but bravado, of course. I didn't have the first clue about what came next.

Ivy found a way, didn't she? So could I.

"This is breaking your mother's heart. I hope you know that."

The last gasps of a man who knew he was losing. Using Mom as a last-ditch effort. "Is there ever going to come a time when you stop using her against me?" I folded my arms, sitting on the edge of the desk. "Why don't you tell me how you feel about this, instead? Do you even care?"

"Of course I do. What do you think this has all been about?"

"I'm not talking about legacy or trusts or newspapers. I'm asking what you think, how you feel. Why is that so difficult to explain?"

He barked out a disbelieving laugh. "Come on, son. How many times have I opened up like that with you or vice versa?"

"I tried the other day," I reminded him in a quiet voice. "When we first talked about what needed to be done. I tried to tell you what that would mean to me, letting her go. And you acted like it didn't matter. What was important to me could not possibly have mattered less to you."

"We can't always do exactly what we want to do."

"I get that, but this isn't a tantrum, like you call it. I'm not doing any of this on a whim. Dad... I love her." There it was. I had never spoken those words out loud and didn't know they were about to pour out of me until they were hanging in the air.

He closed his eyes, releasing a long breath. "I was afraid you would say that."

Now that it was out, I couldn't hold back the words. "She is the most exceptional person I've ever met. I didn't think there were people like her in the world. Shouldering the kind of burden that was left on her. Does she sit around and feel sorry for herself? Hell no. She gets out there and kicks ass, but she fights all alone. I can't protect her. It fucking kills me, to be honest. I've never felt…"

I'd already said too much. He was looking at me like I'd grown another head. I should have known this was a waste of time, but no, I had to try one more time to get through to him and make an asshole out of myself.

"Finish the thought," he implored in a low voice. "Go ahead. Get it all out."

"I can't help her. She won't let me help her. This job was all she had. Not only because of the money and paying her mom's bills but because she loves it. She loves her people. That's what she calls them. She's like the den mother, looking after everybody, helping them become who they want to be. That one girl, Molly, who hurt herself during the retreat, Ivy convinced her to go back to school at night and helped her get into a program. She's constantly playing peacemaker, constantly working to get better at what she does. How can you throw a person like that away?"

He rubbed his jaw, wearing a sheepish expression. "I hear you." His hand dropped and slid into his pocket as he asked, "What about you?"

"What about me?"

"Did she help you become who you want to be?"

He would have to ask a question like that since his favorite hobby was putting me on the spot. There was no time to play dumb and pretend I didn't understand what he meant. "I know who I want to be, and it is because of her. She opened my eyes to the world, the real world, not the one you gave me. I know how lucky I am. I don't take it for granted. I did, but not anymore. And I have her to thank for that too. I didn't plan on this," I admitted, laughing at myself while my soul threatened to shred. "But that's how it is."

"Nobody ever plans on this," he pointed out, slowly walking across the room, stopping in front of the windows overlooking the city. "What to do?"

I decided to jump on the question regardless of whether or not he meant it. "You can start by finding room for the Jones people here. If there's no room in digital media, fair enough. What about all of the other departments on the other floors in this fucking building? You can't find something for them here? Give them a choice, at least. If they want to take their severance and run, they can go ahead. I hate to see them kicked out on their asses. They did work hard."

When he left me hanging for much too long, I threw my shoulders back, standing. "They're my people too. Not just Ivy's. I want what's best for all of them."

"What did you say?" He looked over his shoulder, his brows drawn together over narrowed eyes.

"You heard me. They're my people." Saying it again solidified it in my head. It felt right. "And I want what's best for all of them. The other divisions can do whatever they want. I don't give a shit. This is *my* division."

"All of a sudden?" He eyed the box on my desk. "It doesn't look like you give much of a shit right now."

"I'm revising my terms," I offered with a shrug. "Take it or leave it. If you want me to stay, they're staying... if they want to. And I will work with them to find the right position in the company. We'll restructure our division if we have to. There are areas where we could expand."

"You drive a hard bargain." He turned, his mouth twitching as he looked me up and down. "I have to say, I'm surprised. This is a side of you I didn't expect to meet."

"I would tell you who you have to thank for that, but I'm sure you already know."

His face fell, lines deepening between his eyes. "You know I don't approve of this."

"You know I don't care."

A laugh blurted out of him. "I know. That's the worst part." He inclined his head, adding, "You might not believe it, but I gave a lot of thought to what you said a couple of days ago. How a man my age should understand there's more to a person than where they were born and who they were born to. I have to admit, as much as it pains me to say it, you made a good point. When I look at it that way, I have to apologize for underestimating Ivy. Clearly, if she could have this effect on you, she is a special person."

"I'm glad to hear you come around, though it's not like it matters anymore," I admit. It wasn't easy to confess my defeat. I was not practiced at it, but there's no sense in avoiding reality, no matter how crushing it might be. "As far as she's concerned, I never existed."

"I find that hard to believe. She may act that way now, but I doubt she's really given up."

Were we having this conversation? This wasn't our relationship. Surprisingly, I didn't hate it. There was something comforting about opening up. Even if it was him I was opening up to.

"If she wants the job," he suggested, speaking slowly like the words were too heavy. "I don't see any problem with the two of you being co-vice presidents. It's a little unusual. We've never done it before, but there's a first time for everything."

I had to be hearing things. The man was not suggesting this. I could count all the times he'd compromised in my life on one hand and still have fingers left over. "You're sure that would work?"

He snickered. "I'm the fucking CEO. It will work."

I could also count on one hand the number of times I was genuinely glad to shake his hand. Today was one of them. I crossed the room and clasped his hand, smiling in gratitude. "Thanks, Dad."

"Don't make me regret this," he warned, cracking a grin.

"You won't." Was I telling the truth? I would do my damnedest to make it so.

First and foremost, it meant finding a way to show Ivy how I felt. I would have to take a chance and risk her throwing the gesture in my face, but I needed to try.

"What are you doing?" Dad asked as I sat behind the desk, pushing the box aside and opening my MacBook to pull up the research I'd conducted.

"I might be making a mistake, but we'll have to see." I pulled up a contact number, glancing his way. "If you don't mind, I need a little privacy. If you could have Cynthia send something out to the digital team, letting them know I want to hold a meeting in twenty minutes, I'd appreciate it."

"I'm not sure I recognize you." He couldn't pretend to be upset as he strode from the room. "Not that I'm complaining."

He wasn't alone. I barely recognized myself.

I knew who I wanted to be and couldn't wait to get started.

I could only hope I wouldn't have to be without the woman who made me want to be a better man. I was going to get her back. This time, she would know this was more than a fling. She was never getting rid of me.

20

IVY

Life was a nightmare that insisted on getting worse all the time.

"What are you doing?" I asked, breathless, like I'd just been punched in the stomach. Like I needed this. Walking into Mom's room on Saturday morning, prepared to tell her I'd have to find somewhere new for her to stay, only to find her room being packed up.

"Stop!" I had to get between the aide and the box in which she was packing toiletries. "You don't understand. Or I don't understand, either way. You're kicking her out?" Like I needed this. I was on the verge of collapse as it was, and things kept getting worse. The world spun out of control, and I had nothing to grab onto.

The young aide was about as clueless as the rest of the people she worked with. "I don't know," she mumbled, shrugging. "They told me to pack her things up. They didn't tell me why."

"I'm going to talk to somebody about this, dammit. I pay the bills on time. If you're kicking her out, I want a reason." I looked at Mom, fighting to understand. *God, I did pay all the bills, didn't I? I'd been so busy at work.* "Did they say anything to you? Why are they doing this? Nobody called me!" I was losing it. It was official. This was the last straw.

"All they told me was I wouldn't be here anymore. I thought you knew something." Mom's chin trembled as her eyes filled with tears. "What am I going to do? Where am I going to go?"

Good question. The same question that had been ringing out in my head since I walked into the room to find it in disarray. "I want the administrator. I don't care if she's not here on weekends," I barked at the aide, who stood in the corner. "Now!" I shouted when she didn't move quickly enough. My blood pressure was at an all-time high, and every heartbeat was pounding in my head like a bass drum.

She wasn't out of the room before I decided to go with her. "I'll be right back," I told Mom. I was on the warpath, ready to start threatening jobs if it came to that.

I had never seen this level of incompetence, which was saying something considering the company I just left. The sort of company where somebody like Lucian, with no experience at all, could keep their job over an actual, experienced professional. Somewhere where they used people, pumped them for information, and then left them in the cold.

Right, like I needed another reason to be beside myself with rage as I stormed up one hallway and down another, unable to find anybody in an office. What happened if a patient became seriously ill or there was an emergency? Didn't anybody care?

The fact that I couldn't find anyone to vent my rage on—not to mention get a few answers from—had me on the verge of tears by the time I gave up and headed back to Mom's room. The last thing she needed was to see me cry, but I couldn't imagine a scenario in which I didn't eventually break down sobbing. It was a shithole, but it was the best I could do, and now she was out, and nobody would tell me why. How was it even legal to do that?

"I don't know, Mom..." Anything I was about to say died as I rounded Mom's doorway and found her sitting up, chatting with a visitor who sat in the small chair beside her bed.

How did he make my heart skip a beat even after I promised myself I wouldn't let him manipulate me into forgiving him? It had only been a couple of days since we had that terrible fight, and all I wanted was to drink in the sight of him. He and Mom were smiling and turned their heads when they heard me come in.

"Honey, you won't believe it." Mom's face shone, her eyes sparkled, and for a moment there, it was like nothing had ever happened. She was herself, same as she had ever been, smiling radiantly and full of hope. "They aren't kicking me out."

"I don't understand." I was almost afraid to look at him because he was looking at me, and the second our eyes met, I'd be a goner. It had been torture ignoring his calls, forcing myself not to call him no matter how I wanted to. Now, for some reason, we were in the same room and somehow, he had made Mom very happy. "What is going on?"

"I think I can clear it up." Lucian grinned at Mom before explaining, "I've arranged for your mother to receive care at a top-rated nursing facility in Manhattan."

"What? How is that possible?" Forget drowning in his eyes. I had way too many other things to think about now, such as where the hell he got off. "You can't just, like, make a phone call and—"

"Except I can, and I did." There was no ego involved there. For once, there was no arrogance. He said it as a simple fact, shrugging, while I gaped at him in disbelief. "There are specifics to be ironed out, but she's paid up for the next year. At that point, we can reassess. She may be able to move up to assisted living, in which case there are half a dozen excellent facilities in the city. It's really all a matter of who can give her the best care."

"It's a miracle," Mom declared, tears spilling down her cheeks. "Honey, are you hearing this? It's a miracle!"

A miracle with strings attached. Did I want to throw my arms around him, kiss his face off, and thank him until I lost my voice? Obviously. I sort of hated that I couldn't accept this gesture openly with my whole heart.

"Can I see you in the hallway?" I asked him. I had to leave the room before my sourness ruined Mom's joy. How could he do this? I fucking told him not to, and he did it anyway. Just another Lucian Diamond special.

As soon as he joined me, I whirled on him, poking a finger at his chest. "How dare you?" I whispered. "What is this all about? What is it going to take for you to understand you can't force your way into things like this?"

"When will you stop being so damn stubborn, Poison?" he whispered back, eyeing a couple of open doors nearby. Like I gave a damn about being nice in public at a time like this, but then he was too important for a public scandal. "It's what you need. I have the resources, and I want to provide them. It's the least I can do."

"You're not wrong about that," I blurted out before snapping my mouth shut. I didn't want him to think I agreed with him or that this was a good thing to do. "You went over my head without talking to me about it. I know you think money solves everything, but it doesn't."

"Are you sure about that? Because where I'm standing, money solves a lot of problems, and you need to stop being afraid of that. I have the money. I was able to get her into the best facility in New York, and I was happy to do it. Do you hear me? Happy. I wanted to do it. Where is the crime?"

"Oh, you did this from the goodness of your heart?"

"Don't do that." He shook his head, folding his arms, wearing a smirk. "There's nothing you can say or do to change my mind or make me second-guess my decision. I did this for you. End of story."

I had to wrap my arms around my trembling body, fighting off bitter, frustrated tears. "And what do I have to do for it?" I asked, cutting to the chase. "Don't tell me there are no strings attached. I'm not naïve."

"You don't have to do anything," he replied, wearing a smile that looked almost sad. "I know what I would like you to do, but nobody's forcing you."

"I knew it."

"Stop fighting." His eyes drifted shut, nostrils flaring as he took a deep breath. "Aren't you tired of fighting? All I want is to give you the chance to live without feeling like you have to fight every day. I would also like to offer you a job."

"You can't be serious. Let me guess. I would have to be your assistant. No, thank you."

"My assistant?" he asked. "I thought you had more imagination than that." His head tipped to the side. "I was thinking we could share the vice presidency."

"This is a fantasy." I had to laugh at his childish idea. "You're still not living in reality. You can't snap your fingers and expect everybody else to fall in line."

Laughter rumbled in his chest. "How come they have already?"

"What are you saying?" I whispered. It was unnerving as hell, knowing he was holding all the cards.

"I'm saying it's already done if you want the job," he

shared. "I have the CEO's approval. Also, you might be interested to know I sat down with each team member who came over from Jones and asked them if they would like to stay in another capacity or if they would rather take the severance package. It was a fifty-fifty split or very close to it. Everybody got what they wanted in the end."

Now that did it. I had to reach out and lean against the wall for support. Was it possible? "Everybody still has a job if they want it?" I whispered, afraid to ask in case this was all a dream stirred up by my overwhelmed mind.

"Yes. Including you. Oh, Poison..." he sighed, "... you have no idea how much I want to touch you right now. I'm aching for you. I wasn't lying when I said I offered my resignation. Actually, I insisted on it," he admitted, wincing. "I was even packing up yesterday, ready to throw in the towel. What was the point of being there without you?"

"You're not kidding, are you?" I touched my head to the yellow-stained wall, reeling, afraid to believe it.

"Hey." He reached out to cup my jaw with one hand. That slight touch set off a growl in the back of his throat as he wrapped his arms around me. It was sudden, but I didn't flinch or pull away. How could I when all I had wanted ever since marching out of his apartment was to be in his arms again?

"I don't know what to think. This is all so overwhelming." I closed my eyes, resting the side of my face against his chest. The tightness I'd been carrying for so long that I almost didn't notice it melted away. I was safe. Thanks to him.

"Does this mean you're accepting the job?" His laughter stirred my hair as he pressed his lips to the top of my head. "I mean, your mom will be right there, in the city. Just a quick ride over to see her whenever you want. You don't even have to cross the bridge into Jersey."

"I don't think I've ever heard anything sweeter than that." It felt good to laugh and better when he joined me. "I really should be annoyed with you for going behind my back with this and for putting me on the spot. You knew I couldn't say no if you went in and saw Mom first."

"Was I a little devious? Maybe," he admitted, kissing my head again, pulling his head back to smile down at me. "Desperate times call for desperate measures, and I am desperate for you. Your happiness, your safety, everything. I want nothing but the best for you, always."

A soft, sheepish grin touched his mouth as he took my face in his hands. "I love you. That's all I know for sure. You showed me the sort of man I want to be, and now all I want to do is find ways to be that guy. Somebody worthy of you. Will you give me the chance? I mean..." He chuckled. "If I can learn to sit through meetings and analyze reports, what can't I do?"

"That is a pretty big deal," I admitted, trying to fight back a smile for the sake of pretending I was seriously thinking it over. Really, what was there to think over? I was back where I needed to be.

"Give me a chance, Poison." His smile faded, replaced by what looked like concern. "I swear, you won't regret it. Let me love you."

I didn't need to hear anything else. Touching my fingers to his lips, I nodded slowly. "That's all I want. I've never been in love before you, Lucian, but I'm all in. I'm tired of fighting it. I love you too." It was hard to get the words out once emotion squeezed my throat.

Not that it mattered. Certain things could be shared without words. He placed a finger under my chin, tipping my head back and lining my mouth up with his while placing a soft, gentle kiss there. The sort of kiss that could have gone on and on and led to so many other things, but we were sort of in public and had other things to consider.

He knew it, too, grinning once he let me up for air. "What do you say we get your mom moved, then continue this at my place?"

"You've got a deal." Still, I couldn't help but give him one more kiss before letting go.

Just because I could.

∽

IT HAD BEEN a long day but in a good way. For once, I was happily exhausted because that exhaustion came from getting Mom settled in at the sort of facility where I wouldn't have imagined her staying at in my wildest dreams. All afternoon, I walked around feeling like I should pinch myself but afraid to. I didn't want to wake up if it was a dream.

It wasn't a dream. It was very real, just like walking into Lucian's apartment was very real with him pulling me into his arms and covering my mouth with his. Consuming me, but that was what I wanted. To be consumed. To give myself over to him after holding back. No more fears, no more guilt. It was the two of us against the world.

He backed me away from the front door, picking me up so I could wrap my legs around him. It was like before, the last time we were here, only this time, there wouldn't be any interruptions.

"What do you want me to do to you?" he asked once we were in his bedroom, where he took me to the bed and laid me out across it. Without saying a word, he started to undress, pulling off his polo and jeans. The whole time, he looked at me, watching as I slid out of my shorts and T-shirt. I was so sure this would never happen again. Now that it was, I wanted to savor every second.

What did I want him to do? There was only one answer. "Love me. Just love me."

"That comes easily, Poison… you live in my heart." It was like he wanted to prove it, crawling up the length of my body, peppering kisses over my skin, then finding my mouth again. Yes, this was what I needed. This was all I would ever need. Ever since that first night, some part of me knew it was supposed to be this way. We were meant to be.

I couldn't get enough of him—the scruff on his cheeks against my skin, his flexing muscles under my hands, and the way he eased me into pleasure, whispering in my ear while he played with me, teased me and built me up. "So sweet. Getting nice and wet for me. Nice and wet for when I fuck you," he rasped, sliding his fingers in and out of my soaking pussy.

"Yes… yes, Lucian…" My head rolled from side to side, my eyes closed, sensation sweeping over me until it was all I knew.

"Is that what you want? Do you want my cock inside you?"

"Yes." I lifted my hips, straining for him. "Please."

"Not yet." Even though he was hard as steel and practically digging into my hip, he chuckled when I whined my frustration. "Not until you come for me, Poison. That's all you have to do. One little orgasm. Can you do that?" he asked in his deep rumble of a voice, breathing hard in my ear.

Could I? I didn't have a choice. It was building so fast, bigger and bigger, so big it overwhelmed me. I rode his hand, working with him until it all was too much. I could only squeeze my legs shut, clutching him close as I came hard enough to make my ears ring and my heart damn near explode. The waves went on and on, finally slowing until there was nothing but small aftershocks left.

His lips brushed my skin, his chest heaving, his body so warm and so perfect. Rolling me onto my side so I faced him, he draped my leg over his hip. Then, all at once, he was inside me, filling me, reminding me I was no match for him. For this. This all-consuming, earth-shattering connection.

I stared into his chocolate eyes as he moved, taking me slowly and going deep. The late afternoon sun streamed in, turning his skin to gold and bathing us in warm light as we made love.

My body sang thanks to the way his hands moved over me, teasing me from ankle to earlobe. I was lost in sensation, my whole body, one throbbing nerve that pulsed to the rhythm of his deep, sure strokes. "I love you," I breathed out, and my heart sang. Would I ever get tired of saying that? No, just like I'd never get tired of his kisses, his soft grunts, and the sounds of him losing himself in me.

"I adore you." He devoured my throat, and I threw back my head, offering more. All of me, whatever he wanted, because he had already given me so much more than I ever knew existed.

I was going to come again, and I welcomed it. "Oh, my God..." I gasped, grinding against him. "Come with me."

He closed his eyes, teeth gritted, and I knew he was close. "Yeah..." he groaned out. "That's right, give it to me..."

I did, the tension exploding in my core, heat flooding me when he gave over and let himself come. There was nothing like this. Wrapped in each other, just the two of us in our own world, coming down from what we could only do together.

He spoke first, his voice low and soft. "I hope you know you have a lot of that to look forward to." He placed slow, soft kisses against my forehead and my cheeks before letting out a deep sigh.

I buried my face in his neck, inhaling him while his pulse fluttered against my cheek. "I hope you know I expect it."

"Already demanding." There was a little bit of a growl in his voice. He pulled his head back, smirking. "Not a day into this relationship, and you're demanding sex."

Winking, I replied, "Would you expect anything else?

EPILOGUE - IVY
SIX MONTHS LATER

"It is so generous of you to have us over for dinner like this." I meant every word, though I was afraid it came off sounding trite and empty when faced with the sort of splendor the Diamond family lived in and the elaborate meal that Connor and Pepper Diamond had put together for me.

To think Lucian grew up this way. I had only ever seen this sort of wealth and luxury on a screen. At least before I became involved with Lucian. He had treated me to a look at how the other half lived—an impromptu shopping trip to Beverly Hills on the private jet and last-minute box seats to the hottest show on Broadway, all because I'd told him I liked one of the actresses in the play. So many expensive, exquisite meals. Throwing around cash meant nothing to him so long as he knew it made me happy, and when it came to Mom, he was still going above and beyond. Thanks to the top-of-the-line facility he'd arranged for Mom, she was thriving. She was making friends and even showing cognitive improvement under the care of the doctors and specialists he provided.

But this? He might as well have grown up in a museum. Gorgeous art covered the dining room walls from floor to ceiling, almost concealing the silk wallpaper behind it. There was marble underneath my feet, and the high ceilings made the space feel more like a cathedral than a home. There were breathtaking views from every window—the dining room looked out over Central Park, for instance. The apartment's historic charm had been left untouched, something that did my heart good as I admired the fireplace behind the dining table and the intricately carved mantle on top of it.

Pepper bustled around the table, adjusting the flatware and lighting taper candles that made the crystal stemware sparkle and gleam. A gorgeous floral arrangement sat in the center of the rectangular table. The aroma of roses and gardenias hung in the air and mixed with her citrusy perfume as she walked past.

"Oh, this is nothing," she assured me, wearing a bright, welcoming smile that instantly melted the layer of ice that had formed over my body as we rode up here in the elevator.

Though it wasn't Pepper I was afraid of. Her warmth melted the ice, but it wasn't enough to calm the worst of my fears.

The fact was, though Lucian and I had been working beautifully together, there was still something that always tickled the back of my mind. What did his father think about me? Sure, Connor was nice in the office—pleasant and professional. He offered praise when it was due—not all the time, which meant those rare moments meant that much more. They felt earned.

Still, I wasn't naïve. I knew how the world worked, and I knew Connor hadn't intended to keep me with the company in the first place. He had been completely prepared to throw me overboard, even after my success with the retreat and even after the results my team had achieved.

So, there was always something unspoken between us, and it was obvious he felt its presence. The way he refrained from making eye contact for more than a heartbeat before looking away. The strained smile on the rare occasion when we would pass each other in the hall. Sure, I could have brushed it all aside and told myself this was the side effect of our personal and professional lives intermingling.

He knew Lucian and I were together, obviously, so I told myself that was where the discomfort came from. Like he was overcompensating, making sure nobody thought I was getting special treatment.

I could understand that. If only I believed it was the complete truth.

Connor's footsteps rang out, growing louder as he approached the dining room after he and Lucian had peeled off to find the perfect bottle of wine to go with our chateaubriand, which now glistened enticingly on the table. "I think this will do," he announced, holding up a bottle of red.

I didn't bother asking for the brand or the vintage since I wouldn't have known the difference, anyway. I could only follow his lead, the way I followed Lucian's lead on so many things that were outside my realm of experience. Considering where I came from, that meant just about everything.

Lucian followed close behind him, and the sight of his knowing grin let me breathe easier. Clearly, he and his father had shared a brief, private conversation while going through the family's extensive wine collection.

Pepper ran a hand over her gray streaked curls like she was making sure she was in place too. I hoped by the time I was her age, I looked half as good—fit, trim, and energetic with hardly a line on her dewy skin. "Terrific. I'm starving, and the catering service worked so hard on this meal. We should enjoy it, right?"

I also appreciated the way she didn't bother pretending she put all of this together on her own. "*Mom's greatest talent has never been in the kitchen,*" Lucian warned me on the way to the penthouse. There had been nothing but fond laughter in his voice. "*I mean, she makes a mean pot of pasta, but something tells me she's going to want to impress you tonight.*"

The fact that somebody like her wanted to impress a nobody like me left me feeling a little overwhelmed. I hoped I was hiding it as Lucian pulled out a chair for me. While Connor uncorked the wine, I offered, "Mr. Diamond, like I was telling your wife, this is so generous of you. Thank you."

His soft laughter preceded a gentle hand wave. "Nonsense. For one thing, while you're here, you can call me Connor. We don't have to be formal."

"The same goes for me," Pepper added as she took her seat across from me, winking.

"You want her to call you Connor?" her husband asked, laughing as she swatted at him with the back of her hand. Funny, but that simple exchange went the rest of the way toward easing my apprehension. Seeing Connor out of the office, without his professional façade in place, was damn refreshing.

"She knew what I meant," Pepper insisted while I nodded, giggling. "Ivy is part of the family now. It's only right."

Lucian grinned at me as he reached for a big bowl of salad. "I like the sound of that," he murmured, and we exchanged a look that spoke volumes. These six months had been a dream like every wish I'd ever made in the deepest depths of my heart came true. It wasn't always easy. It wasn't like deciding we loved each other meant all of our conflicts were magically resolved, and we would never rub each other the wrong way again.

But now, when we inevitably caused friction, it was almost sort of fun to work it out, especially when our arguments ended with at least some of our clothes dropping onto the floor.

"Yes, and it's taken too long for us to have this dinner. Ivy, I apologize," Connor murmured as he plated thick slices of chateaubriand for the four of us. "I hate to offer up the usual excuse of life being busy and everything else getting in the way, but I assure you, this has been on my mind."

"There's no need to apologize," I told him, even if his words meant so much. I was sort of wondering, even though I hadn't brought it up to anybody. Not even to Lucian. Would we ever clear the air completely? Or would it be assumed that we were on good footing, that we could move on from our past complications?

"I think there is. And so does my son," he added, smirking at Lucian as he handed him a plate. "And he's right. I was a fool, plain and simple."

"Is somebody recording this?" Pepper whispered, checking under the tablecloth like she was looking for a microphone.

"I'm glad my wife finds this so funny," he continued, giving her the sort of exasperated look that came from decades together. "But I'm serious. I lost sight of what truly mattered. When a man reaches my age, and it's clear he needs to think about his legacy and what he's leaving behind, it's only natural for him to be a little…"

"Pigheaded?" Lucian suggested, and I kicked him under

the table, but he pretended not to feel it.

"I was going to say overly cautious," Connor retorted, rolling his eyes as he sat once we were all served. "I turned into someone I always told myself I would never become. I was looking at numbers alone. Forgetting about the people behind those numbers. I'm sorry. Really, I am." As he spread a silk napkin across his lap, he added, "And I'm grateful to my son, the smartass he is, for opening my eyes. I also got a little too rigid in my thinking. I needed someone younger and more creative to come up with a solution that kept everyone's jobs in place." Finally, his gaze landed on me again. "You've done remarkable work. I've gone out of my way to be fair in the office. I don't want anyone thinking it only takes sleeping with the boss's son to earn accolades."

"Charming," Pepper whispered, snickering.

Connor scowled lovingly at her before continuing. "Now we're alone, the four of us. I can be more open with my praise. Together, the two of you have ushered in a new era for the company, and that's the way it should be. We need to be able to move into the future. I can finally say with complete confidence that we're on the right track, and that's thanks to you."

"Wow, Dad," Lucian breathed out. It wasn't often he was stunned into silence, but this was one of those times. He must not have expected to hear that kind of praise tonight. For me, sure, and I knew he was happy to hear it. But for himself?

"I mean it," Connor told him, his tone softening along with his gaze. He wasn't a boss anymore. He was a father, proud of his son. "I feel confident when I think about stepping back and handing over the reins. I know you have what it takes to maintain our legacy... no, to improve upon it."

Under the table, Lucian reached for my hand and gave it

a squeeze. I squeezed back, my heart too full for words. It was everything I had ever hoped to hear and so much more. Because it wasn't all about me, it was us, Connor's faith in both of us. Watching the love of my life glow under his father's praise, there wasn't a doubt in my mind he would've sworn only months ago that he didn't need it, but I knew the truth. It meant the world, knowing he had his dad's blessing.

"I think this calls for a toast." Pepper wiped a tear from the corner of her eye, lifting her sparkling crystal goblet. "To the future of Diamond Media, but more importantly, to the future of the Diamond family." Again, she winked at me, and I knew without being told that I was included in that statement.

I had never wanted so much to be a part of anything in my whole life.

Once we toasted and sipped the incredible, rich wine, we settled into our meal. No sooner did Pepper pick up her knife and fork than she asked, "So, when can we expect to hear wedding bells for the two of you?"

Lucian almost choked. So did I. "There I was," Lucian mumbled after gulping water. "Thinking we had crossed the last hurdle."

"Oh, son..." Connor chuckled, exchanging a knowing look with his wife. "This is as good a time as any to find out the goalposts are always shifting. Wait until she starts pestering you for grandchildren."

Lucian choked for the second time in less than a minute, and my face went redder than the wine in my goblet. Yet somehow, it felt right—, maybe as right as anything had ever felt.

THE END.

READ THE EPIC FINALE NEXT...

As the heirs reunite for a big day, trouble brews beneath the surface. Can they survive the storm, or will everything they've built come crashing down?

Preorder Endless Love today!

BONUS SCENE

Don't want to let Ivy and Lucian go just yet?

Grab the FREE bonus scene here:

https://BookHip.com/HCFARMJ

ALSO BY MISSY WALKER

ELITE HEIRS OF MANHATTAN SERIES

Seductive Hearts

Sweet Surrender

Sinful Desires

Silent Cravings

Sensual Games

Endless Love

ELITE MEN OF MANHATTAN SERIES

Forbidden Lust*

Forbidden Love*

Lost Love

Missing Love

Guarded Love

Infinite Love Novella

ELITE MAFIA OF NEW YORK SERIES

Cruel Lust*

Stolen Love

Finding Love

SLATER SIBLINGS SERIES

Hungry Heart

Chained Heart

Iron Heart

SMALL TOWN DESIRES SERIES

Trusting the Rockstar

Trusting the Ex

Trusting the Player

*Forbidden Lust/Love are a duet and to be read in order.

*Cruel Lust is a trilogy and to be read in order

All other books are stand alones.

JOIN MISSY'S BOOK BABES

Hear about exclusive book releases, teasers, discounts and book bundles before anyone else.

Sign up to Missy's newsletter here:
www.authormissywalker.com

Become part of Missy's Facebook Reader Group where we chat all things books, releases and of course fun giveaways!

https://www.facebook.com/groups/missywalkersbookbabes

ACKNOWLEDGMENTS

Thanks for reading Sensual Games. If you've read a few of my books, you've probably noticed that the enemies-to-lovers trope is my favorite to write. Maybe it's because, like Ivy, I've dealt with misogynistic, self-entitled men in the workplace myself. Before my writing career, I had a male boss who felt threatened by me—and I made sure to show him exactly what I was capable of!

A huge thanks to my editors, Chantell, Kay, and Nicki, for your invaluable feedback, and to my amazing betas, Ella, Karmin, Maria, and Saskia, for your patience and support.

To my fans, especially my Facebook reader group, Missy Walker's Book Babes—building this community has been incredible, and I love everything you share.

Much love,
　　Missy x

ABOUT THE AUTHOR

Missy is an Australian author who writes kissing books with equal parts angst and steam. Stories about billionaires, forbidden romance, and second chances roll around in her mind probably more than they ought to.

When she's not writing, she's taking care of her two daughters and doting husband and conjuring up her next saucy plot.

Inspired by the acreage she lives on, Missy regularly distracts herself by visiting her orchard, baking naughty but delicious foods, and socialising with her girl squad.

Then there's her overweight cat—Charlie, chickens, and border collie dog—Benji if she needed another excuse to pass the time.

If you like Missy Walker's books, consider leaving a review and following her here:

instagram.com/missywalkerauthor
facebook.com/AuthorMissyWalker
tiktok.com/@authormissywalker
bookbub.com/profile/missy-walker

Printed in Great Britain
by Amazon